Part of the Team?

By four-thirty, Michelle was dead on her feet. But she'd never felt so good about a practice. Or a team.

"That's it for today," Coach shouted. "Good job. Remember practice is the same time, same place, every day."

Michelle pushed her sweaty bangs off her forehead. Her legs felt like wet noodles. All she wanted to do was collapse, but now all the boys were heading out the side door with Coach.

Quickly, Michelle scrambled after them.

"Hey, wait for me, you guys!" She caught the back of Kevin's shirt. Stupid move.

Kevin whirled. "Wait? You can't go with us."

"Why not? I'm part of the team."

Kevin's laugh echoed in the hollow gym. "Hey, guys, don't hit the shower yet. We've got Smidge here trying to crash our locker room!"

WHO LET GIRLS IN THE BOYS' LOCKER ROOM?

by

ELAINE MOORE

Rainbow Bridge
Troll Associates

LIBRARY OF CONGRESS CATALOGING-IN-PUBLICATION DATA

Moore, Elaine
    Who let girls in the boys' locker room? / by Elaine Moore.
        p.   cm.
    Summary: When Michelle starts sixth grade at the local junior high school, she's elated to have a chance to play basketball on the boys' team until she finds out that the boys don't want girls on their team.
    ISBN 0-8167-3439-9
    [1. Basketball—Fiction.   2. Sex role—Fiction.   3.   Schools—Fiction.]   I. Title.
PZ7.M7832Wh   1994
[Fic]—dc20   94-820

For Coach Jim Lewis and the girls in his summer basketball camp; Jeanne Daunorus, Fairfax County, Virginia, P.E. teacher, who taught me boxing out; and particularly Coach Nichols, my eighth-grade basketball coach.

For truly incredible eyes, apply two coats of mascara," Sandy said.

Michelle Dupree sat cross-legged on her bed, surrounded by sports magazines and the basket of laundry her mother had asked her to fold and put away. No problem. Her mom and dad wouldn't come home from the store for at least another two hours. Besides, she had more important problems to worry about. Nervously, she fingered the knob on her new combination lock while her best friend, Sandy, read the instructions on a tube of mascara.

Michelle and Sandy lived on the same block. They had known each other ever since Sandy gave Michelle a shampoo using green finger paints in kindergarten. Tomorrow they would start Jefferson Junior High together. The combination lock was for Michelle's locker. The mascara was for Sandy's soon-to-be truly incredible eyes.

"Right. And for a truly incredible combination lock, turn twice," Michelle mimicked. As long as she lived, she'd never get the hang of this blasted lock. Whoever invented them ought to be arrested. Disgusted, she fished a Nerf ball off the rug and tossed it at the miniature basketball hoop attached to the back of her door. *Swish.*

If Sandy's mother suspected her daughter had used the money she was supposed to spend on school supplies to purchase a tube of velvet black mascara—and actually planned to wear it tomorrow, in public—she would kill Sandy, no questions asked. If Mrs. Vacaro knew Sandy also planned to smear something called Ooh-La-La on her lips, she would not only kill her daughter, she would cremate her and toss her ashes to the wind.

This was exactly why Sandy was applying both mascara and lipstick for the first time in Michelle's bedroom. It was also why Sandy had begged Michelle practically on bended knee to carry both the mascara and the Ooh-La-La lipstick tomorrow in *her* purse.

It was what best friends were for.

Michelle bent over a square slip of paper and tried for the umpteenth time to concentrate. The code for the combination lock was printed in tiny black letters.

"Left to sixteen," she muttered under her breath. She turned the knob slower. When it came to combination locks, Michelle had three thumbs.

She started to say as much. Then she glanced up and saw Sandy wasn't doing much better with the mascara.

"It's not fair," Michelle said. "We shouldn't have to worry about dumb stuff like mascara and combination locks. We shouldn't even be going to Jefferson. At least, not this year."

Precisely one month and two days ago, Michelle's dream bubble had burst. She'd probably never recover.

8

For as long as Michelle could remember, she'd wanted to be a BIG sixth grader at Seneca Ridge Elementary. This was important for someone who had always been the shortest kid in her class. Then the school superintendent's office made the fateful announcement. Certain elementary schools in their district had grown too crowded, and budget cuts prevented building new classrooms. The problem had to be solved by having some sixth graders attend middle school with seventh and eighth graders. Seneca Ridge Elementary was on the list.

Instead of finally making it as a mighty sixth grader, Michelle was stuck being an eleven-year-old, four-foot-eight dink.

Worse, she'd be an eleven-year-old, four-foot-eight dink in a school loaded with seventh and eighth graders who couldn't stand the thought of breathing the same air as lowly sixth graders.

Michelle knew all of this from an authority: her older brother, Brian. Brian was entering eighth grade at Jefferson. The way he'd acted when he heard the superintendent's decision, you would have thought Brian's life was in jeopardy instead of Michelle's.

Michelle had no idea what her parents said to Brian to make him understand the consequences of such an important decision upon Michelle's entire life. Whatever it was, it must have worked.

Taking pity on her, Brian thoughtfully drew a spectacularly detailed map of the entire junior high, including all three floors, two wings, and the secret elevators no one else was supposed to know about.

Even though a map of their new school had been included in the big white orientation envelopes both Michelle and Sandy received in the mail, Brian's was way better. His was color-coded and included such important landmarks as bulletin boards, hall clocks, water fountains, vending machines, and the tunnel to the underground swimming pool.

"Don't even bother with that other map," he told Michelle. "Jefferson is so big and confusing, a little kid like you could get lost really easy. Look, I've drawn arrows where you're supposed to go. I even put an X where you report to homeroom. Use this map and you've got it made, Sis."

Like Santa Claus and the Tooth Fairy, sometimes big brothers could surprise you.

"Okay. What do you think?" Sandy turned around. She held the pink tube of mascara in one hand, the wand in the other. Her eyes were only half open. They appeared weighted down by black fuzzy caterpillars.

"No. Don't tell me," she said before Michelle had a chance. "I'm only a quarter of the way there. You're supposed to do the underside of your upper lashes first. From the roots to the tip in one long sweep. When that coat dries, you do the topside and then . . ."

"You sound like my dad when he's painting the bathroom."

Sandy started to giggle. "Now look what you made me do!" Black streaks pointed down both cheeks. "Thanks to you, I've got to start all over."

"Big deal." Michelle tossed a pair of socks into the basketball net. "I've tried this stupid lock at least ten times. I can't keep my hands from shaking, I'm so scared. You should have heard what Brian told me last night. I would have called you, but it would have given you horrible nightmares."

Sandy slid a bunch of magazines off the bed and sat down, anxious.

"The eighth graders take the sevies. Those are the seventh graders," Michelle explained in case Sandy didn't know. "And they duck the sevies' heads in the toilets. And then . . . the eighth graders . . . FLUSH."

"FLUSH!" Sandy shrieked.

Michelle nodded. "Flush."

Sandy shook her ponytail furiously. "I don't believe it. They'd get expelled."

"Brian swears it's true. And if that can happen to seventh graders, just imagine what could happen to us."

Michelle picked a pair of socks out of the laundry basket and rolled them up. "And then," she said, throwing the little white ball in a high arc, "there's Bip Day when the eighth graders get to tweak the sevies' ears. What will they do to us?"

"I don't know."

"If you ask me, the sevies are lucky. They only have to worry about the eighth graders."

"We got seventh *and* eighth graders."

"Brian says we are dog meat. Ground dog meat."

"Well, I for one am going to think positively," Sandy said, returning to the mirror. "I'm concentrating on all the new clothes we got and also . . ." Sandy opened up the tube of mascara. "Think of the new guys we're gonna meet."

"Huh. Like they're really going to care about sixth graders. Besides, how can you even think about boys at a time like this?" Michelle flung her lock down on the bed. "We're going to have to take *showers* at Jefferson. For P.E. we have to get undressed in front of a bunch of other girls and we get graded for doing it." Michelle looked down and sighed. "I was definitely counting on having another year to grow."

"Me, too," Sandy said miserably. "At least we share the same homeroom. That reminds me, what are you going to wear?"

Before Michelle could answer, the bedroom door popped open. There, framed in Michelle's doorway in all his eighth-grade glory, stood Brian holding a Frisbee. Beside him, jumping around like a hairy maniac, was Hercules, the Duprees' gigantic golden retriever.

"Fetch!" Brian let the Frisbee fly, aiming for Michelle's bed. When Hercules landed, magazines and laundry scattered everywhere. The combination lock fell to the floor with a loud thud.

"Brian!"

Brian banged the door behind him. "It's your turn to walk Hercules. If you know what's good for your bedspread, you'd better hurry."

Michelle cringed. The only thing louder than Brian's idiotic laughter was the sound of his sneakers thumping down the steps like a herd of stampeding elephants.

Quickly, Michelle grabbed her Rollerblades and the leash Brian had hurled in her room after the Frisbee.

"C'mon," she yelled at Sandy. "It's almost time for me to fix dinner, anyway. Hercules and I will skate you home."

Sandy slipped the mascara and lipstick in the purse on Michelle's dresser. "Okay, but whatever you do, don't forget your purse tomorrow."

"Don't worry," Michelle hollered over her shoulder as she and Hercules bolted down the stairs. "My map is in there. I wouldn't dare forget it. No way do I want to get lost on my first day of junior high."

CHAPTER 2

The next morning, Michelle stood in front of the mirror and worked her blonde hair into a French braid. She fluffed her bangs. They were too long.

Why hadn't she cut them last night? Why hadn't she let her mother take her to Hair Affair? Why hadn't she tagged along with Sandy and her mom when they went to Geoffrey's Salon?

She didn't need anyone to remind her. She'd had other things to do. Her parents' store, for example—a rental business in the middle of town. Her father liked to say that running a successful family business took teamwork. That's why, for as long as Michelle could remember, both she and Brian helped out with odd jobs. They worked through the summer vacations without complaining—too much.

Of course, their parents didn't believe in all work and no play. Sometimes, Michelle rode her bike to the community pool. After she swam laps, she came home and bounced her basketball in the driveway and shot hoops until dinner.

But getting a haircut never had been high on her list of priorities. Not like the store or any activity involving sports— most particularly, basketball.

Michelle lived for basketball.

For the past two years, she had played basketball for the Astros on the Turnpike Girls Youth League. Okay, so she was short. So what? She made up for her size with incredible speed. Michelle was so quick, she left most mosquitoes in the dust.

The only time Michelle didn't think about the game was when she was sleeping. Then she dreamed about it.

First, there were the sounds. The *pa-boom-pa-boom-pa-boom* as she dribbled across the honey-colored floor in the Community Center or the blacktop pavement in her driveway. *Boom* was the ball smacking the ground; the lighter *pa* was her fingers tapping the ball's pebbly surface. *Pa-boom-pa-boom-pa-boom.* She liked the high crack when the ball hit the hoop's wire rim. She liked the deep rumbling drum when it banged the backboard. Most of all, she liked the *swish* when the ball fell cleanly through the net.

Then there was the fast action of the game—racing down the court to score a goal, jumping in front of the girl you were guarding, sliding across the floor. She loved all of it, especially when the Astros won—which they did often enough so that she had trophies lining her bookcase to prove it.

Basketball was the only thing she could look forward to now that she was stuck going to Jefferson Junior High.

"Are you sure you don't want me to drive you to

school on my way to work?" her mother called from the kitchen.

Michelle opened the door a crack and hollered downstairs. "No, thanks. Sandy and I are taking the bus."

Michelle double-checked to make sure she had Sandy's makeup and her map. Then, after putting her purse on her shoulder, she hurried downstairs.

"Don't worry, Mom," Brian was saying. "She'll be okay. I drew her a detailed map. Besides, the cheerleaders will be wearing their uniforms and helping the new kids. If Michelle gets lost, she can ask them."

"Right, Mom," Michelle said brightly. "It's not first grade. It's junior high."

Saying the words *junior high* sent Michelle's stomach into a tailspin. She faked a smile as she bravely headed out the door. She could see Sandy waiting on the corner.

Earlier than Michelle would have liked, their bus arrived. With a loud *whoosh,* the doors opened their big rubber lips. Brian and the rest of his eighth-grade friends climbed on first, followed by a group of sevies. Michelle gulped and trailed on last, after Sandy. It took every ounce of courage to keep from turning back. And then the doors closed behind her with a *swoosh.* She was trapped.

When the bus arrived at Jefferson, Michelle stared through the window at the sprawling school. She'd seen it plenty of times before—mostly when she'd gone to Brian's football games. But that was at night. Now, in the light of day, Jefferson Junior High appeared bigger than ever.

"Michelle!" Sandy shouted. "Are you all right? You look positively green."

"I am."

"Fine, but whatever you do, don't throw up! Here, follow me."

Michelle tried to grab onto Sandy, but it was like trying to grab a bobbing raft in the middle of a hurricane. As they started up the school's steps, Michelle was swept up in a sea of bodies.

Out of the corner of her eye, she saw teachers standing on the front walk, shouting directions, and cheerleaders in perky sweaters and pleated skirts. In that brief instant, Michelle lost sight of Sandy. And Brian. There wasn't a single person she recognized.

Feeling no bigger than the tiniest grain of sand, Michelle was caught up in a whirlpool and swept into the hallway. She felt herself being pushed, banged, turned around. Everyone else seemed to know where they were going.

Brring! The bell practically screamed in her ear. Like magic, the waves of bodies disappeared, sucked into their proper classrooms. Michelle leaned against the wall, too stunned to move. Where was she supposed to go? And then she remembered: Thank goodness she had Brian's map!

Michelle took a deep breath and opened her purse. Being careful that Sandy's mascara and lipstick stayed buried at the bottom, she slowly pulled out the map and unfolded it. She'd have to remember to thank Brian. This map was going to make her day.

Okay, so the front doors were behind her. With the arrows Brian had drawn, finding homeroom would be a cinch. If she hurried, she could get there before the teacher called roll.

With the map in front of her face, Michelle turned right under the clock and zipped down a hallway, counting three doors as she did so. Past the water fountain on the left. Gaining confidence, Michelle jogged down the ramp, accelerating once she found the second water fountain. Just one more left, then two doors on the right and a sharp turn into homeroom.

"Whew!" Michelle blew her bangs off her forehead and kept going. She could never—ever—thank Brian enough.

With one hand, Michelle opened her purse. No sense letting everyone else in her new homeroom know she had to depend upon a color-coded map to find her way around junior high.

Ooof!

Just as she turned the corner, she ran smack into what felt like a brick wall. Papers and books flew through the air. Her purse fell with a crash, sending everything rolling—pens, pencils, *everything* . . . including a certain pink container and an embarrassing tube of Ooh-La-La.

When Michelle looked up, she was staring into the brightest, bluest eyes she'd ever seen in her entire life. They twinkled under a shock of sunny blond hair that belonged to what had to be an eighth grader. Her head barely reached his shoulder.

Michelle continued to stare dumbly while a girl's voice echoed through the hallway. "What do we have here but a little sixth grader trying to sneak into the boys' locker room!"

Michelle blinked. The voice belonged to a cheerleader in a blue and gold pleated skirt. Obviously, she was talking to the brick wall—er, boy—Michelle had collided with.

"Give her a chance, Stef. She's a little lost pigeon," the boy replied.

Confused, Michelle scanned her surroundings. The cheerleader wasn't kidding. Michelle had almost walked straight into the boys' locker room!

That Brian! What a mean joke. Worse, like a dummy, she'd fallen for it. Sometime—sooner than Brian would like—she would kill him for sure! Meanwhile her things, including Sandy's makeup, lay scattered all over the place.

Michelle's face burned with embarrassment. Quickly, she tried to grab everything and cram it back into her purse. Great! The boy, whoever he was, was trying to help. If he reached the mascara and lipstick before she did . . .

"Oh, what do we have here?" the cheerleader said in the snidest voice possible. "Something for truly incredible eyes. And look at this, Derek! It's Ooh-La-La, high gloss, no less!"

Michelle gulped. She snatched the makeup from the girl's hand. "It's not mine. I'm keeping it for a friend."

"Oh, Derek! Isn't that cute? This little sixth grader is babysitting makeup for another itty-bitty sixth grader."

"Stef, cut it out! It's her first day. Where are you supposed to be, Smidge?"

Michelle couldn't decide whether she should be angry at the new name, with its obvious reference to her height, or happy that at least someone in this monstrous junior high was showing kindness and sympathy. It didn't matter.

She needed directions—and fast!

By the time Michelle finally limped into homeroom, Sandy was already seated.

"What took you so long?"

"Tell you later." She'd barely dropped into the chair Sandy had saved for her when the bell rang for the next class.

Michelle's shoulders slumped. It didn't take a brain surgeon to know this was going to be a very long day.

For the rest of the week, Michelle focused on only one thing—survival. At times, she felt like she was racing through a maze blindfolded as she tried to make friends and keep in contact with Sandy. Unfortunately, the only classes they shared were homeroom and English. At least they had the same lunch period, although it wasn't easy trying to find each other in the huge and crowded cafeteria.

It was during lunch that Michelle saw Skye Davidson, a willowy girl with long chestnut hair, wandering aimlessly around the cafeteria with her lunch tray. Sandy noticed Skye at the same time.

"Who's that girl?" Sandy asked. "She's gorgeous. I'll bet she's a fashion model. Too bad she doesn't have a place to sit."

Michelle stood up, hoping Skye would see her and join them. "Her name's Skye and she's not a model. She's in most of my classes. Her family just moved here. I don't think she has many friends."

"What are you waiting for?" Sandy gave Michelle a

hard nudge. "Wave her over!"

A few minutes later, Skye slid her tray on the table beside Michelle's. "Thanks for letting me sit with you."

The lonely way Skye said it caught Michelle by surprise. It must have caught Sandy by surprise, too. Right away, Sandy exploded into a wild one-way conversation about makeup, hairstyles, clothes, and boys.

"Which reminds me," Sandy said when she finally stopped to take a breath, "are you going to the football game Friday night? We are. Everyone is."

Skye took a nibble out of her sandwich and put it down. "I don't think my parents will let me. I'm not allowed to go places by myself."

"No problem. Tell your folks to come," Michelle said. "They can bring you and stay for the game. My family wouldn't miss a Jefferson football game for the world—especially now that my brother, Brian, made first string."

Sandy raised her eyebrows. "Right. Football's a big thing around here. All the parents and practically the whole town come to the games. Except this year we absolutely cannot sit with our folks. According to my magazines, that is *so* geeky."

Skye leaned forward to look past Michelle and blink at Sandy in disbelief.

"Geeky as in freaky," Sandy explained, in case Skye didn't understand. "One thing you don't want is to be geeky or the eighth graders will flush your head in the toilet."

Skye's face paled. For a moment it looked like she might faint dead away.

"Gosh, I really feel out of it," Skye said in a hushed voice. "My last school was an all-girl academy. We used to lock people in the bathrooms, but we never flushed. And in my whole life, I've never been to a football game. I did play basketball in P.E. class, though."

Michelle perked right up. Maybe there was hope for Skye after all. "Oh, you played basketball!"

"Only in P.E. and I was a real klutz."

"Hey, you guys," Sandy interrupted. "It's not basketball season. We're talking football here. You know, with guys!"

Michelle turned to Skye. "Anyway, check it out with your mom and see if you can meet us there. Tell her we're expecting you."

"Right," Sandy agreed. "We'll wait for you by the snack bar."

Finally, it was Friday—the last day of a truly awful first week—and the night of the Jefferson Eagles' first football game. From the bleachers Michelle, Sandy, and Skye had a good view of everything. Down below, the cheerleaders waved their blue and gold pompoms and shouted into megaphones.

"Give me an E. Give me an A."

The girls helped the crowd spell out "Eagles," the team name. Michelle made sure that Skye stood up and cheered with the rest of them as the band played the school song and the boys ran out on the field.

Sandy pointed to the line of cheerleaders. "I bet the girl in the middle, Stephanie, is the captain. She's cute. Popular, too."

"They're all cute," commented Skye. "I could never jump like that in front of all these people."

Michelle barely heard. "Give her a chance, Stef." The boy's words echoed in her ear. Sure enough, Miss Bouncy Flouncy, Captain of the Eagles Cheerleading Squad, was the very same person who had made the snide remarks outside the boys' locker room.

Suddenly, the crowd was standing again as the Barracudas kicked off to the Eagles.

"GO-O-OO, TEAM!"

During the game, Michelle noticed someone from league basketball. The Awesome Keisha, an African-American girl who played for the Hornets, stood down front, looking very cool in a white oversized T-shirt, black jeans, and matching sneakers.

When Keisha turned around, Michelle waved. Their eyes caught and Keisha smiled. Michelle counted how many years she'd played against Keisha's team. Keisha must be in eighth grade.

At half time, the Eagles and the Barracudas were tied, 6-6. But in the third quarter, the Barracudas let loose. The Eagles ended up losing the game, 32-6.

Michelle was watching Stephanie bounce around as if she didn't understand the final score when Michelle's mother tapped her on the shoulder. "Sweetie, Dad had to move the car. Go tell Brian we're parked beside the cafeteria entrance."

Wow! Michelle could hardly believe her luck. She raised her eyebrows at Sandy and grinned. What a perfect opportunity for revenge!

"Quick, Sandy, give me your program! I'm going to fix Brian good for that awful map trick." She yanked a pen out of her purse.

While Sandy and Skye looked on, Michelle drew a bunch of arrows and silly signs on the program.

"This is going to be so great," she told Sandy. "Plant your lips here." She pointed to a spot on the paper.

"Kiss the program?" Skye shrieked.

"You don't know her like I do." Sandy tapped her forehead with her finger. "The girl is bonkers."

"Hurry up!" Michelle urged. "It's a map stupider than Brian's. I need lip prints on it like a big smoochy kiss."

Giggling, Sandy blotted her lips on the program.

Perfect! If Michelle had tried, she couldn't have planned it better.

Leaving her friends and holding the program behind her, Michelle squeezed through the gate and onto the field. Brian had his back to her as he stood alongside Number 9, the Eagle quarterback.

Michelle screamed as loud as she could. "Brian!" When she was sure both boys had heard, she began babbling in high-pitched singsong baby talk. "Bri-Bri! Mommy said to tell you Daddy moved the car-car." Michelle waved the program in the air, hoping to attract as much attention as possible.

Brian turned around slowly and glared.

"Since you're so good with maps, Bri-Bri," Michelle went on, "I made one especially for you with itty-bitty pictures instead of words."

She thrust the map at Brian, ready to embarrass him

in front of his teammate.

"See, Bri-Bri." She smacked the program with her finger. "All you have to do is follow the arrows to the big red smoochy . . ."

Just then Number 9 turned around. Michelle sucked in her breath. The map fell to the ground. Number 9 was the brick wall, the boy with the blue eyes she'd bumped into on her way to the boys' locker room.

If only the football field would open up and swallow her whole. If only a giant meteorite would drop out of the sky and crash into the goal posts. If only . . .

But none of that happened.

Instead, both boys came closer. Her only hope was if Brian's friend didn't recognize her as the lost sixth grader outside the boys' locker room. Michelle's knees wobbled.

"Hey, don't I know you from someplace?"

"I doubt it, Derek." Brian smirked. "This is my *baby* sister."

Derek was just about the cutest thing she'd ever seen and Michelle didn't even like boys. He was holding his helmet against his hip. Then he bent down to pick up the map.

All the breath left Michelle's body. Wasn't it bad enough that he had heard her talking baby talk? Did he have to see her map with the big red smooch?

"Maybe not," Derek went on, apparently not noticing how her heart was about to pound right out of her chest. "But like I was telling you," he said, handing the program to Brian without bothering to look at it. "Those Barracudas better be ready because I'm gonna get them under the net."

It wasn't until Michelle got back to the car that Derek's words sank in. What was he talking about, Michelle wondered. "Under the net" was a basketball term.

"Brian's on his way." She climbed into the back seat. "He's really in a bad mood," she warned her parents, just in case Brian blasted her for trying to embarrass him in front of Derek. "It's probably because they lost. You'd think it was the championship." Michelle shrugged. "They can still get the Barracudas in their next game."

"Not this year, Sweetie," her father said.

Michelle frowned. "What do you mean? We always play the district teams twice."

"Not this year." Her father leaned his head back so she could hear. "Budget cuts, remember? Unfortunately, the football schedule was cut in half. There are rumors circulating that other teams will be affected, but no one knows the details yet."

Michelle rested her elbows on her knees and stared glumly out the window.

Funding problems. She was sick of it. That's why she was stuck at Jefferson. Those stupid budget cuts had better not interfere with her playing on the school basketball team. So far that was the only neat thing about Jefferson. She'd never played on a school team before.

Michelle nibbled nervously on the tip of her braid. What a silly thing to worry about. Budget cuts could never affect the basketball team—could they?

CHAPTER 3

Monday morning was a regular mob scene. Michelle and her friends couldn't get past the main lobby because of a crowd of excited kids.

"Kevin. Rocco. Please, stop shoving," Ms. Cramer, a school counselor, called—not that it helped.

"Hey, what's going on?" Michelle shouted.

"Whatever it is, Derek and Stephanie wormed their way to the front." Sandy turned to Skye. "Can you see what's on the bulletin board?"

Skye cleared her throat and began to read.

"This year only one basketball team will represent Jefferson Junior High." She paused to gulp nervously. "Boys and girls wishing to try out for the Eagles should report to the gym Wednesday after school."

"Hey, Skye, you ought to try out." Michelle had to yell to be heard over the shocked reaction of the crowd. "As tall as you are, you'd be great snagging rebounds."

Skye leaned down toward Michelle. "I'd be too scared. Besides, I already told you. I'm a natural klutz."

"No, you're not," Michelle said quickly. "Besides,

everyone's going to assume that you play basketball anyway. Come on," Michelle urged. "Try out with me so we'll be together. You can come over to my house and I'll help you practice. It'll be fun."

Skye took a deep breath. "Okay, but only if you're absolutely sure."

Just then, Sandy jabbed Michelle in the ribs. "Watch out. Here comes Stephanie, draping her many arms all over poor Derek like a lovesick octopus."

Poor Derek was obviously enjoying himself. A strange anger seethed inside of Michelle.

"What kind of girls would want to play on a team with boys? Is B.O. required?" Stephanie asked in her usual snotty voice.

Michelle whirled. "Me, that's who," she heard herself say. "I'm trying out for the Eagles. You can just watch me."

Stephanie tossed her head. "Is the little smidgen sixth grader still trying to get into the boys' locker room?" she said loudly so everyone could hear.

The news traveled fast. By noon, the only kids who didn't know that Michelle "Smidge" Dupree—sister of the almighty Brian, owner of truly incredible eyes, and wearer of Ooh-La-La lipstick—had decided to go out for the Eagles basketball team were the lucky kids who were home sick in bed.

Midway through the afternoon, Sandy passed Michelle a note.

28

*Michelle—Are you sure you know what you're
doing? The boys are going to hate you! If they
don't squash you first.*
    Sandy

"I'm not worried about boys," Michelle said as she
and Sandy ambled toward the buses after school. "I'm
worried about Bigmouth Brian. Imagine what he'll tell my
folks if he gets to them first."

Sandy's forehead wrinkled with concern. "Excellent
point."

Michelle nodded. "It's a good thing he has football
practice. Instead of going home, I think I'll walk to the
store. My folks will still be there."

"Smart. You can casually bring it up."

Casual? Around her mother, who had a nose like a
private investigator? Michelle left Sandy in the bus line
and marched down the sidewalk, rehearsing to herself
what she would say to her parents. She had to be good.
She needed their support.

"Hi, Mom!" Michelle breezed into the store, dropping
her books on the counter like it was the most natural
thing in the world to stop in after school.

"Michelle? Sweetie? Is everything okay? Are you feeling all right?" Mrs. Dupree left the cash register and came
around to the front.

"I'm fine, Mom. I just thought I'd stop by and see how
things were going."

Mrs. Dupree gave Michelle a suspicious look.
"Everything seems to be running fairly normally. It's

Monday so your father is in the back unloading chairs from the van."

"He must miss having Brian around to help."

"Maybe, but I bet he'd be glad to see you. Why don't you go back and say hello."

"I will in a minute."

It amazed Michelle how many people rented tables and chairs on weekends. On Fridays her father spent practically the whole day loading chairs in a van and taking them to people's houses, only to have the chairs come back again on Monday. The same was true of punch bowls and fancy silver.

"Your classes went well today?" Her mother flipped through a stack of receipts.

"Yeah, fine. We have our first math quiz this week."

The bell to the shop dinged as old Mr. Higgins came in to return the same weed trimmer he rented every weekend.

"Hello there, little lady," he said to Michelle as she wrote up his ticket. "Did I ever tell you I had a yellow canary the color of your hair?"

Michelle smiled at the nice old man. At least he hadn't called her "Smidge."

"I think maybe you told me a couple of times."

"Well, there, you see," he said, waving as he left.

Michelle recorded the amount in the book the way her mother taught her before punching the numbers into the cash register.

"The *Journal* is on the counter." Mrs. Dupree pointed. "Your league schedule is printed inside. Looks like another full basketball season."

"Mom," Michelle blurted. "About basketball. The Eagles have a pretty good team. The girls' team stunk, but last year the boys almost made it to the championships."

"Oh? Maybe they'll both make it this year."

"That's the thing." Michelle bit her lip before continuing. "Mom, there's only going to be one team on account of, you know . . ." Michelle hesitated before saying the awful words. "Budget cuts."

Her mother's arms wrapped around her. "Oh, honey, I'm sorry. I know you wanted to play for the Eagles."

"No, Mom. It's okay. Really. I'm going out for the boys' team."

Her mother stepped back. "You're what?"

"Well, not exactly," Michelle said carefully. "I mean it's no longer the *boys'* team. It's the *Eagles*."

"But . . ." her mother gulped.

"Mom, don't you see? This could be the greatest thing that ever happened to me. Think of the opportunity. You know how I've always wanted to play basketball with boys."

"Sweetie." Mrs. Dupree placed her hands on Michelle's shoulders. "Have you thought this through? You could get seriously hurt. An elbow in your eye or . . ."

"Mom, nothing bad is going to happen," Michelle reassured her. "It's perfectly safe. If it wasn't, they wouldn't allow it in the first place."

"But, Sweetie," her mother insisted. "You're already on a team. What about the Astros?"

"That's a *girls'* team, Mom. This is the *school* team. If I have to go to junior high as a sixth grader, I'm not going to

31

sit by and watch everyone else have a great time. You said yourself that I should join some clubs, get the team spirit, so I would feel better about being at Jefferson. Well, I'm not exactly the club type, and the clubs at school are totally boring. I'd rather play on a real basketball team with a bunch of boys."

"There are other girls doing this?" Mr. Dupree asked.

Michelle whirled. Her father had been standing behind her, holding a soft drink in his hand and listening the whole time.

"Sure," she said, thinking fast. No way would her parents let her play if she was the only girl on the team. "There's a tall girl, Skye, who'd really be great with rebounds. The girls who played on last year's team will probably try out. And there's this other girl I know from league basketball. She is totally awesome. Her name is Keisha. I'll bet you anything she tries out."

Mr. Dupree popped open the soda. "Honey, I'd give it some extra thought if I were you. Basketball is a contact sport."

"That's what I tried to tell her," Mrs. Dupree said. "But now that I think about it, Michelle *has* been playing one on one against Brian in the driveway ever since she could bounce a ball. Maybe she should go for it. After all, those budget cuts weren't her idea."

Mr. Dupree gazed helplessly toward the ceiling. He put his arms out and Michelle slipped inside like a flash. "Give it all you've got, Sport."

Next Michelle had to deal with Brian.

Normally, Brian didn't get home from football practice

until five-thirty, leaving barely enough time for a shower before coming down for supper. Tonight, Brian was late. They had already set dinner on the table when he walked in.

"Have a good practice, son?" Dad passed the mashed potatoes in Brian's direction. It looked like Brian had gotten hit with a couple of hard tackles. The side of his face was bruised.

"Yeah, we did, but I wasn't late because of practice. I had to set some kids straight. You wouldn't believe the rumor going around school." He glared at Michelle.

"Get this, Dad," he said, plopping heaps of potatoes on his plate beside two chicken drumsticks. "You would not believe how stupid some kids can be. And, Mom, you know those tabloids they sell at the grocery? Well, apparently they aren't the only experts at spreading gross and exaggerated lies."

Mr. Dupree raised his eyebrows. "Brian, do you want to explain or are we all supposed to sit here and wait for you to tell us that someone in your school discovered Elvis Presley in the biology lab?"

Brian rolled his eyes. "Okay, you asked for it. The rumor at school is that Michelle is trying out for the boys' basketball team!"

"Is that all?" Mr. and Mrs. Dupree said together.

Brian almost dropped his drumstick. "Is that all?"

"Brian," Michelle said with feigned sweetness. "It's not a rumor."

"WHAT!" Brian leaped to his feet.

Mr. Dupree rarely yelled at the table, but he yelled now. "Brian, sit down!"

Brian sat.

"Somebody please pass the peas," Dad barked.

As soon as her parents weren't looking, Michelle stuck out her tongue at her brother. "Phony map-maker," she hissed. If she had only known how mad she could make Brian by going out for the basketball team, she would have tried out for football.

"I can't believe it." Brian shook his head numbly. "My little sister is trying out for the boys' basketball team."

It was time to set the record straight.

"Brian, it's *not* the boys' team anymore. Get with the program. If I want to play basketball for Jefferson, there's only one team I can play on. I don't have a choice."

"Yes, you do," Brian said smugly.

"Name it."

"Stick to the girls' league where you belong."

"WHAT!"

"You're butting in where you're not wanted."

It wasn't what Michelle wanted to hear.

"I might not even make it," she said quietly. "I mean the guys who played last year will be going out."

"Most of those guys are in high school now. It's just Derek and a couple of others, and he expects to be captain."

"Derek?" Michelle almost dropped the dishes she was carrying into the kitchen. "The quarterback?"

"Yeah, big eighth-grade Derek," Brian said, following behind her and setting his dishes on the counter.

"Look, Michelle," he said, lowering his voice. "I just don't want to see you get hurt. You're not exactly big for your age. And if you think girls can be mean, you should hear what the guys are saying about you. I can't always be there to protect you."

"I don't need your protection," Michelle snapped.

"Fine, but remember, I warned you," Brian said. "There have never been girls on the boys' team before. Coach Hatchet-Face isn't going to like it. He likes to win and everybody knows you can't win with a bunch of giggling girls on the team. Hatchet-Face will take care of you, Michelle. You and any other girls stupid enough to try out for the Eagles."

CHAPTER 4

Tweet!

All activity in the gym stopped as Coach Hawkins' smooth brown face looked up from his clipboard. "Hustle up!"

Michelle pushed her way through the crowd, pulling Skye along with her, until they were standing beside Keisha and right in front of Coach. With her shoulders slumped and arms dangling helplessly, Skye looked as lost as Michelle had felt on the first day of school.

"Whatever you do, don't leave me," Skye whispered urgently.

"He's probably going to run us through a bunch of drills and exercises to warm us up," Michelle whispered back. "Just stay with me."

No sooner had she said that than the gym door swung open. In pranced the cheerleaders, Stephanie leading. Michelle groaned. Great, just great. Was no place safe from Stephanie?

A group of guys in the back started to grunt. A loud wolf whistle echoed through the gym, followed by another loud TWEET!

"More of that behavior, young man, and you are out of here. Got that?"

"Yes, sir."

Michelle counted fifty-seven kids trying out for the team, most of them sixth graders who didn't know how tough basketball could be. The kid who had let out the whistle was an eighth grader named Kevin. Judging by his Eagles T-shirt, Kevin had been on the team last year and should have known better, the creep.

Keisha covered her mouth with her hand and leaned closer to Michelle. "It looks like our Dream Team has to share the gym with a bunch of whoop-de-doo cheerleaders," she whispered.

Michelle nodded and made a face. She hoped it wasn't always this way.

Except for Keisha, the girls who showed up for try-outs were a bunch of what Brian called "giggly-poos." Skye towered over everyone except Coach, while Michelle was the smallest.

Coach told them to spread out. Just as Michelle expected, they started by stretching their hamstrings and quadriceps. Next, Coach began jumping jacks. His arms went over his head, hands meeting in a loud clap as his legs went out. The rest of the group did the same.

"One, two, three, four. Two, two, three, four."

Everyone moved in synch. "Five, two, three, four. Six, two, three, four."

At the other end of the gym, the cheerleaders practiced leaps. Stephanie was up front, bouncing all over the place in her sweater.

Michelle looked down and almost fell over.

She didn't have much but what she did have jiggled in an embarrassing way. She felt her face heat up and quickly closed her eyes, wishing she could die on the spot. Maybe none of the boys had noticed.

TWEET!

Next, Coach had them run backward the whole length of the court. Then forward and backward again. Forward and back.

TWEET!

"On your own. Grab a ball. Move, move, MOVE!"

Keisha moved faster than any of the boys. Before Derek could pick up a ball, she dribbled down the court and sank a basket. Michelle saw the startled look on Derek's face as the ball went in.

"Good shot!" a boy named Matt called out.

A minute later, Derek flashed by with his shirt off. Michelle's knees turned to jelly. Shooting a basket was the last thing on her mind. The next thing she knew, she was flat on her behind.

Quickly, she scrambled to get up before Coach noticed. No such luck. Hatchet-Face beamed right in on her. She knew what he was thinking: Cross Smidge off the list.

TWE-E-E-E-ET!

He motioned with his arms and, once again, everyone ran toward him. Fifty-seven pairs of sneakers squealed to a screeching halt.

"Let's change the pace a bit. Sit down right where

you're standing. I've got something to say before we start up again."

Michelle dropped in her tracks with Skye beside her.

"Take a good look at yourself. See how you're sweating and breathing hard, huffing and puffing like old men and women. It takes wind to play basketball. You have to be able to sprint. It takes strong legs." Coach seemed to be staring at Michelle's toothpicks. "You have to have stamina at the beginning and the end of the game. You have to move, move, MOVE!"

Keisha had gone into a trance, lapping up Coach's every word.

"You've got to work at it. Some of you might want to play basketball in high school or get college scholarships. That's okay. Some of you want to be the best. But are you willing to lift weights? Are you willing to run till it hurts?"

In a single fluid motion, Coach arched the ball into the air and through the net. *Swish.* It never touched the backboard. Never touched the rim.

"Right there, that's the easy part."

The silence was deafening.

He let the ball bounce once and picked it up on the second bounce. "College scholarships? They only take the best. And for this Eagles team, I'll do the same. Only the best. So if you want to quit, go ahead. I'll work you hard and in the end" —He bounced the ball on the floor— "I'll only take the best.

"Your moves have to be automatic. For those of you who think basketball comes naturally, I'm telling you, you're gonna run, you're gonna sweat. You're gonna have blisters. I'm gonna be in your worst nightmares. Playing *good* basketball takes work. Now who here feels like they're in shape?"

Michelle glanced around, expecting Derek to leap to his feet. But he just sat, his arms wrapped around his knees, waiting. Before she knew what had happened, Michelle stood facing the Coach.

"Way to go, Short Stuff," Keisha shouted.

It made her feel a little odd, getting a cheer from an awesome eighth grader like Keisha, but there wasn't time to think about that now. Instead, Michelle ran her fingers through her bangs, pushing them off her forehead. She crouched down with her arms spread wide. She saw Coach's mouth twitch slightly, the steely glint in his eyes.

"It's the moves. Watch the moves," Coach shouted to the rest of them. "I've got to keep the ball. She's gonna try to steal it and I'm gonna move the ball." He danced away, dribbling closer to the net.

"C'mon, c'mon," he urged Michelle.

"Go for it, Short Stuff!"

Michelle went lower, thrusting her arm out, trying to take the ball away. He pivoted. She threw up her arms, trying to block. The ball went in.

"That's strong opposition," he said. "Now we go for teamwork. Listen up. We two are on the same side now. I'm going in for the basket. Always assume that the ball is going to miss and rebound. That means you throw up those arms and jump for all you're worth. You want that rebound, you gotta call for it first."

Together Michelle and Coach worked the ball down

the court. She bounce passed it to Coach. He threw toward the basket and the ball bounced back off the rim.

"Mine!" he shouted. "Got it!" He grabbed the ball, leaping again to sink it into the net.

"Good moves," Coach told her.

Michelle nodded, embarrassed, then turned and walked back to where she'd been sitting.

Next, Coach set up drills in different parts of the gym. Some kids dribbled in a line. Others took layups and practiced foul shots. Michelle grimaced as a giggly-poo sent a ball sailing over a basket and her silly squeals filled the gym.

"Air ball!" some boys yelled, laughing.

Just when Michelle thought she was doomed to take foul shots forever, Coach motioned her over to join Matt and a bunch of other boys in a mini-scrimmage under the net.

She'd played basketball with guys before, sometimes shooting hoops, sometimes one on one, sometimes a real game on the playground or at the Community Center. But she'd never played with a coach watching. She'd never competed in team sports with guys. Mentally she ordered her hands to stop perspiring. She told her stomach to turn right side up and her heart not to stop beating until they finished.

She, Matt, and a big guy named Rocco were on one team, up against three guys she didn't know. They'd play half court.

Rocco started at center. When Coach handed him the ball, Rocco dribbled once, twice, and shot the ball so hard at Michelle it almost knocked her down. Right away, the opposition zoomed in on her, arms waving, voices challenging. She pivoted, kept her cool, and bounce passed the ball to Matt, who dribbled it in for a layup.

"All right," yelled Keisha. "Good play!"

The next time they had the ball, Rocco tried shooting from outside the key. Like a flash, Michelle darted under the basket, expecting the rebound.

Bam! The ball hit the backboard.

Arms up, Michelle flew after the ball like she'd been shot from a rocket. The next thing she knew, she was sitting on the floor again, seeing stars.

"What happened?"

Matt was sprawled on the floor beside her. He held his head with both hands. "Oooh. I thought girls were supposed to be soft."

TWEET!

"Did I hear anyone call for the ball?"

"No, sir," Michelle and Matt answered weakly.

"Take a break, you two. There's ice packs in the refrigerator in my office." He pointed to the tiny room connected to the gym. "I don't want to see either of you back on the floor for at least ten minutes. Got it?"

"Yes, sir."

They began walking toward Coach's office. Then Matt stopped. "There's no sense both of us going. Why don't you sit down in the bleachers. I'll get the ice packs."

Skye hurried over. "Maybe we should go home," she said, sounding concerned. "Do you want me to call your mother?"

Michelle pressed the ice pack Matt handed her to her forehead. "No! This is basketball! Now get back there before Coach catches you goofing off."

Reluctantly, Skye wandered off to join the other kids.

"Man, talk about a goose egg," Michelle said to Matt. "I'm going to have a big one."

Matt grinned. "Sorry."

She laughed. "You're sorry? For what? I should have called for the ball."

"Well, I am sorry you got hurt. You went up so fast. I never saw anyone move as fast as you."

"Except maybe her." Michelle motioned toward Keisha, who bounded down the court, madly dribbling the ball behind her back and between her legs.

"Yeah, she's great, isn't she? She played on the girls' team last year. I bet she ran buckets around all of them."

"The league team she plays on is pretty tough. We had a rough time beating them."

Matt looked impressed. For a seventh grader—and a boy—he almost seemed nice. "You both played in the same league? No wonder you're trying out. That's pretty neat."

"Yeah, but I don't know if we'll make it. I guess nobody knows." Michelle sighed. "I got off to a pretty lousy start. I just hope Hatchet-Face doesn't think this is how I play the game—on my bottom."

xcept for Brian's radio, the house was quiet. Michelle's eyelids barely fluttered. Judging by the clock on her night stand, it was eight o'clock—but A.M. or P.M.?

Suddenly, Michelle remembered. She had totally crashed after that killer basketball practice. If her mother called her for dinner, she hadn't heard. She never even bothered to change out of her shorts and sweaty T-shirt. Yuck!

Michelle struggled to her feet. At the same time her math book hit the floor with a thud. Michelle grimaced. Tomorrow's math quiz.

Still groggy, Michelle picked up the book and looked in the mirror. The knot on her head from where she'd banged into Matt was a good one. Cute.

Hoping her mother had saved her some dinner, Michelle padded downstairs in her sweat socks. She found a note on the counter.

Michelle—Dad and I went jogging with Hercules.

Dinner is in the fridge. Pop it in the micro, two min-
utes on High. Be back soon. Mom

Michelle stood in front of the open refrigerator and groaned. She never noticed how bright the light was before. Keeping her eyes open was an excruciating experience. Maybe she should put ice cubes on her forehead.

She pulled her dinner plate from the refrigerator. The pork chop did look good. If only her head didn't hurt so much.

Once when Brian came home with a black eye, Dad placed a piece of raw meat against Brian's face. The pork chop wasn't raw but . . .

Michelle pressed the pork chop against her forehead. Not bad. The pain more tolerable now, she sat down at the dining room table and opened her math book. She was still holding the pork chop against her forehead when Bigmouth came clomping down the stairs.

"Hey, what's that on your face?"

Michelle tried to dodge Brian's hand but she wasn't fast enough.

"Would you look at that zit!"

"It's not a zit, Sweat Breath!" Michelle's temper flared. "I banged into Matt at practice."

"Well," Brian said, standing back to get an eyeful, "that's one way to knock out the opposition. Boom! Crack!" He smacked his hand in his fist. "Maybe you should start wearing my football helmet. You didn't kill the other guy, did you? What's his name? Matt?"

"Yeah, Matt. And, no, I didn't kill him and, double no,

I don't need your helmet. Besides, it's too icky-sticky from that glue you put on your hair."

"Gel, Michelle."

"Glue on you, Brian."

"You know that bruise is changing colors, don't you?" Brian said, unable to keep his big mouth shut. "By tomorrow your whole face will be a weird shade of purple. By the time you get to school, you'll look like a California Raisin."

"Lay off."

Brian wouldn't. He pulled up a chair.

"Hey, anyway, about your practice. Derek says Keisha is a regular bomber."

"Derek?"

Brian rolled his eyes. "Derek?" he mimicked in a ridiculous falsetto. "Yeah, Derek. Thanks to you stupid girls, he can hardly think about football and we've got a big game coming up. You girls really know how to cripple a school. Kevin is a complete mess, too. Something about a female leaning tower of pizza who's got legs like a spider and hangs around with you."

Michelle sighed. At this rate, she was never going to get her studying done.

"That's Skye. The only one taller than her is Coach Hawkins. And Derek's right about Keisha. She is awesome. When Keisha hustles, which is all the time—I mean, that girl never stops—she makes everyone else look like they're standing still. You should have seen her whizzing around like a shadow in one of those big white T-shirts she always wears. Her T-shirt was so big you couldn't see her shorts underneath—just those pumping

46

legs. She was sinking three pointers like it was nothing."

Just then a flash of gold lunged at the pork chop compress Michelle held against her forehead.

"Hercules! Down!" Dad yelled as the kitchen door slammed behind him. Hercules sat in front of Michelle and started to whine. And drool.

Mrs. Dupree put her hands on her hips. "What in the world are you doing with your dinner?"

"It's for her zit," Brian informed everyone, sounding perfectly serious.

It didn't take a nuclear physicist to know what Brian's mouth would blab to everyone in school.

"Sweetie?"

She was supposed to offer an explanation. Michelle lowered the pork chop so her mother could see the swelling above her left eyebrow.

"Holy cow! How did that happen?"

"It's nothing, Mom."

"Don't believe her," Brian interrupted. "Our sweet delicate Michelle head butted some poor guy into a coma. You and Dad are probably going to get hit with a lawsuit."

"Shut up." Michelle stuck out her tongue. "Mom, make him stop. It's not true."

"Michelle, why didn't you say anything when you came home? You shouldn't have gone to sleep. Henry?" Mrs. Dupree called her husband. "You don't suppose Michelle has a concussion, do you? Come here and check her while I take care of her dinner. Maybe we should take Michelle to the emergency room."

"Mom! It's no big deal."

Mr. Dupree held up four fingers in front of Michelle. "How many, Sport?"

"Thirteen. Dad! I'm okay. Really."

Satisfied, Mr. Dupree threw his jogging towel on the couch in the family room. Right away, Hercules ran for the towel and began shaking it fiercely. Finally, exhausted, he fell down on the floor with a loud plop and began to snore. If only silencing Brian was as easy.

"Maggie," her father called. "Michelle's fine. You can cancel the trip to the emergency room."

Mrs. Dupree gently squeezed Michelle's shoulder as she set the warmed plate on the table. "Sweetie, the next time you get hurt, I want you to tell me."

"Sure, Mom."

Michelle poked at the pork chop with her fork. Amazingly enough, it didn't look any worse after being used as an ice pack. Was she was onto something? If she decided to go into sports medicine when she grew up, she was going to help her patients plan their meals for maximum benefit.

Nosy Brian was checking out the shopping bags their mother had left on the table. "Mom, you got my stuff. Thanks."

He peered inside a bag and pulled out a pair of white sports socks with red and white ribbing. "All right!" He laid them on the table. "How many pairs did you get? They must have been on sale, right, Mom?"

He tossed the socks in a high pile. Next came a thermos, two T-shirts, a red and white soccer shirt, and a can of tennis balls.

Suddenly, Brian frowned, obviously puzzled. He

pulled a strange white stretchy thing over his head and turned to their mother.

"Thanks, Mom. My helmet was slipping around and messing up my hair. I guess this thing is supposed to keep my helmet in place."

"Brian!" Mrs. Dupree laughed. "Don't you know what that is? Oh, of course, you . . . I mean, I guess I'm glad you don't know. . . ."

Mrs. Dupree dissolved in a fit of giggles while Brian looked from her to Mr. Dupree, the white thing still on his head.

"Sure I do, Mom. See, you pull these handles down." Brian pulled the white straps that dangled beside his ears. "They probably wind around somehow. Um, does this come in sizes? Maybe you got the wrong . . ."

"Brian!" Mrs. Dupree spluttered. "You're not the only athlete in the family. That item on your head is for Michelle. It's a sports bra."

"It's a what?" Brian yelled, yanking it off his head.

Michelle's mouth dropped. So did her father's.

"For our Michelle?" Mr. Dupree asked.

"Yes, Henry. She needs it."

"A sports bra?" Brian shouted, holding it in front of his nose. "It looks more like . . . like . . . a slingshot." Before Michelle could grab her bra out of Brian's hand, he positioned a tennis ball inside the bra and shot it into the family room.

Sproing!

"Mom!"

"Brian!"

49

"Hercules, no!"

"E-nough!" Mom yelled at Brian. "Now put that thing down, apologize to your sister, and go to your room. Immediately!"

"Okay, okay. Sorry, Michelle."

She could hear Brian laughing all the way upstairs. Now she supposed he'd tell all of his friends, including Derek, that his sister wore a slingshot.

"What's the big fuss?" Mom asked. "For pete's sake, you'd think I'd bought her a jockstrap."

"Mom!"

Fortunately, the phone rang, sparing Michelle from having to listen to any more embarrassing conversation. Michelle grabbed the stupid white stretchy thing and stuffed it in her pocket. How did she get stuck in this crazy family?

"Skye, you have no idea! You have saved my life!" Michelle said into the telephone. "This whole house has gone totally bonkers because my mom bought me a sports bra."

"She did? Are you going to wear it?"

Michelle put her hand in her pocket. "I guess. I sort of have to."

"Oh." Skye paused. "The reason I called you is because my entire body aches and I was wondering, since I found two tubes of that muscle stuff that football player advertises on TV, do you suppose it's safe to use, or is it only for old people and football players?" she asked breathlessly.

If Skye didn't sound so serious, Michelle would have laughed. "Haven't you ever strained your muscles before or gone out for team sports?"

"No, and I wouldn't have this time except you asked me to. I'm not especially coordinated."

"You're not so bad," Michelle said. "You kept hitting your big toe whenever you dribbled, but we can work on that. I still think you've got great potential. Why don't you come home with me tomorrow on the late bus? We'll work on your dribbling before final cuts on Friday."

"Okay, but don't get your hopes up. It won't do any good. I'm not going to be able to move tomorrow anyway. I wouldn't even bother going to school if it wasn't for that math quiz."

"The math quiz!" Michelle shrieked. "I haven't even cracked my math book."

When Michelle hung up the phone, her mother's eyes could have thrown daggers.

"A math quiz tomorrow and you haven't studied?"

"It's not a big test," Michelle tried to explain. "It's only a quiz and I've been trying to study. See, here's my book," she said, holding it up.

"Michelle, I was under the impression that we had an understanding about this studying and sports business," Mom said. "Your homework comes first. It's the same with Brian. We do have our priorities. If it's going to be too much to play both in the basketball league and also on the school team while keeping your grades up, then something will have to go—and it's not going to be your grades. It will have to be the league team."

Michelle bent over her plate and poked at the cold food. She was almost too tired to chew. Certainly, she was too tired to argue with her mother.

She thought it was interesting that her mother automatically assumed she would make the Eagles. Was she that good? What did Coach think? Or did all parents just naturally assume that their kids were better than anyone else's?

Finished with dinner, Michelle grabbed her math book, trudged upstairs, and flopped on her bed. She stared at the poster of Michael Jordan hanging on her wall. "The Higher the Goal, the Higher I Fly," it said. She propped her knees up and flattened the math book against her legs.

First things first. Tomorrow morning, the math quiz. Tomorrow afternoon, tryouts—second round.

CHAPTER 6

Just as Michelle expected, every day fewer kids showed up for tryouts. She could hardly blame them. Coach made the training rigorous. Day and night, his voice pounded the walls inside her brain. If you wanted to make *his* team, you had to work, work, WORK and move, move, MOVE. Only the strongest would survive.

Now, it was Friday—the third and final day for tryouts. Michelle was hanging on by a mere thread. The Awesome Keisha, of course, was still her usual dynamite self.

Amazing! The girl never faltered. Watching her was magical, like observing the pros. Even when Keisha practiced under a hoop by herself, she danced on the soles of her feet, dribbling, always glancing over her shoulder, feinting and fighting with an invisible opponent.

What a difference between her and Skye.

Michelle sighed. She hoped she hadn't done the wrong thing by encouraging Skye. If Skye didn't make the team, she might never try out for anything again.

As planned, yesterday she and Skye had ridden the late bus home. She showed Skye some dribbling techniques and watched as Skye dribbled the length of the driveway several times without stopping. When Skye had enough confidence to switch hands while keeping the ball in motion, Michelle stood under the basket and yelled, "Not bad. Now try for a layup."

Pa-boom-pa-boom-pa-boom. Skye dribbled waist-high. She moved the ball closer before coming to a dead stop under the basket. A long second passed as she stared at the net without moving.

"Go for it!"

Skye missed the basket, but then she caught the rebound flat-footed and sank it.

"Way to go, Skye!" Michelle yelled.

Skye grinned. "I got it! Wow! This is great."

Skye threw the ball again. *Swish!* Michelle couldn't help laughing, seeing Skye enjoy herself.

"I'm glad you talked me into trying out," Skye said when they stopped for a water break. "Even if I don't make it, I still had fun."

"Don't ever say that," Michelle answered sharply. "You have to think like a winner. Play like you've already made the team and you *will* make it, Skye."

Skye slid her ponytail holder out of her hair and on to her wrist. She shook her head. "I don't think so."

"That's definitely the wrong attitude. Do you know what the pros do?" Michelle went on. "They imagine themselves winning. You kind of play a video inside your head where you're making all the right moves."

Skye giggled. "You are nuts!"

"Just try it," Michelle said, standing up.

So here they all were on Friday afternoon—their last chance before final cuts. Michelle had already bitten all ten fingernails down to stubs. Who was she kidding? She was as nervous as Skye.

"Listen up," Coach hollered. "I want you to spread out in smaller groups. Move, move, MOVE!" he shouted.

Michelle raced with a group of guys·to an area on the far side of the gym to practice her foul shots. Naturally, Keisha was already ahead of them and shooting baskets.

"Hey, maybe we ought to play shirts and skins." Acting macho, Kevin swaggered over to a group of girls. "So who's gonna be on my team?"

He threw his shirt on the sideline, raised his eyebrows, and whistled. Before Michelle could tell Kevin to drop dead, two other guys threw their shirts down.

"Hey, not you guys, stupid," Kevin said boldly.

"That's gross," one of the girls called out. "Grow up."

Behind Michelle, Keisha tossed the ball in the hoop for a three pointer. "In your dreams, Kevin."

Disgusted, Kevin picked up his shirt and walked off.

Standing at the foul line, Michelle bounced the ball three times and let it fly. *Swish.*

"Way to go," Skye yelled.

Michelle grinned. She hoped Coach noticed how she sank foul shots with almost every throw. Being little, she got fouled a lot when she played league ball. Coach needed to know she took advantage of this by racking up points at the foul line.

She also hoped Coach noticed Skye's obvious improvement in dribbling and how she'd stopped hanging onto

Michelle like a homesick puppy.

TWEET!

"Spread out now. If you want to make the team, if you want to play basketball in the big leagues, you have to be able to handle the pressure. The score's tied. You have eight seconds on the clock. That's pressure."

Coach gripped the ball close to his chest. "You have to move. You have to get the ball down to your court. You have to make the shot in time to make the point. But first you've got to get it down there."

He faked a pass.

The next time, he let the ball go. If Keisha hadn't been watching, it would have hit her in the face. But Keisha caught the ball like it was no big deal and chest passed it back to Coach with an easy snap.

He nodded his approval. "Good move."

"For those of you who don't know"—Michelle noticed his jaw muscles flex as he stared at a giggly-poo—"that was a chest pass."

Some of the girls erupted in a fit of giggles.

Coach turned his back in disgust. "We're going to work on chest passes today. Later we'll do a few lobs, but for now I want you lined up in four groups. Let me see those chest passes."

Another shriek of giggles.

Thank goodness this was the final day of tryouts. Next week Michelle wouldn't have to stomach these goofy girls. Of course, that was assuming she made it through the final cut.

Michelle's eyes swept the gym, searching for Skye.

When she found her, Skye was standing in her usual pose, arms folded, head slightly bowed, waiting her turn in line. She rubbed one foot against her leg, like a stork.

When Skye glanced up, Michelle tapped her head, reminding Skye to think like a winner.

TWEET!

"Hustle up! Come here and sit down."

Skye was jogging toward them when Coach grabbed her elbow. Skye froze. If he let go, she'd probably faint dead away.

"We're going to do some guarding here. Listen up."

He turned to Skye and motioned toward the basket with his head. "That's your goal. Go for it." In the same split second, he stepped back and chest passed the ball to Skye. Immediately, he dropped into a guard's crouch.

Michelle closed her eyes and prayed.

"Atta girl, Skye! Do it! Do it!" Keisha roared.

Michelle opened her eyes in time to see the ball fall through the basket.

"That's the way it's done," Coach praised.

Skye breathed a sigh of relief and sat down, all legs.

Coach checked his clipboard and separated them into squads.

First Michelle guarded Matt. Then he guarded her. It was fun working against Matt, who wasn't as likely to call her Smidge or tease her about a game of shirts and skins. She felt scrappier playing against him. She found herself making the same quick moves she did in league ball, only faster, because she felt challenged.

Twice she missed Matt's fake, but the third time she

was onto him and managed to steal the ball just as he was driving in for another basket.

"Good moves," he said when it was their turn to let someone else take the net.

"Thanks. You, too," she said, sitting down comfortably beside him on the sidelines to watch as Coach shot the ball to Derek in the center circle while Keisha waited at the head of the key.

First, Derek pivoted in one direction but charged the other way. Keisha wasn't fooled. She went with him to the basket. When the ball went up, she was there too.

All action in the other areas of the gym stopped as everyone watched Keisha and Derek.

Keisha rebounded the ball and dribbled back to center court. Suddenly, she whirled, put her hand out, and pushed it against Derek's forehead.

Derek glared and grabbed at the ball. Too late. Keisha dribbled in and shot an easy basket.

"Foul!" Derek stormed. But everyone watching only laughed.

That only made him madder. Derek turned up the heat as Keisha thundered the ball toward him. "Your turn, hotshot!"

Derek's feet pounded the gym floor as he sailed toward the net. Arms flashed and the ball went up and bounced off the rim.

Again Keisha rebounded and took possession of the ball. She moved to center court.

"Baby, baby. Come to Mama. Come on, come on," she baited.

She faked to the left and went right, leaving Derek in the dust. Derek's face turned bright red as Keisha flashed past him, then leaped suddenly into the air with an incredible hook shot.

Derek glared at Keisha, then turned and raised his eyebrows at the other guys. He sat down, fuming.

TWEET!

"We need to stop now!" Coach boomed. "We have some players here, specifically Derek and Kevin, who have to prepare for the football game. Good luck tonight, guys."

"Thanks, Coach."

"I'll make the final cuts down to eleven players over the weekend. I want to thank all of you for your enthusiasm and tell you that what I have to do is not easy. I'm hoping to post the list Monday morning." TWEET! "Dismissed!"

Keisha sent a ball rolling across the floor, then ran after it as if she were being chased by an invisible opponent. Without missing a stride, she scooped the ball up and disappeared into the hallway. Michelle figured she was heading for the girls' room. Unable to resist, she trotted after her.

Keisha made eye contact in the mirror as soon as Michelle entered. "So who is Coach picking for his team?"

Michelle blinked. "He said eleven. Derek, for sure. After that, I couldn't say."

"Me neither, but I want a spot on the team with this coach. He pushes me to my limits. I like that."

Keisha turned away to dampen a paper towel. She

folded it and pressed it against the back of her neck. "You hustle good. To look at you, no one would expect you played basketball, but you really knock the socks off some of those guys. You're like a streak of lightning coming out of nowhere."

Michelle gulped at the unexpected compliment. "You know what they call you? The Awesome Keisha."

Keisha let loose with a laugh so deep and genuine it sounded like they might be friends. She patted Michelle on the shoulder. "Well, anyway, I hope you make it. But only if I make it, too."

Now it was Michelle's turn to laugh. She'd never known anyone as totally upfront as Keisha.

"Yeah, me too."

Michelle stuck out her hand, extending her little finger. Keisha did the same. They locked pinkies and pulled.

"To both of us."

"Yeah, good luck to both of us!"

CHAPTER 7

Michelle plunked her tray down between Skye and Sandy in the cafeteria.

"The suspense is driving me wacko," she wailed. "It's like Coach magnetized the bulletin board. No matter what class I'm headed for, it automatically drags me—"

Michelle stopped as Julio Rodrequez came tearing through the lunchroom toward Matt's table. Suddenly, a whole group of seventh-grade boys went berserk, popping lunch bags and tossing milk cartons in the air. Then Matt threw his baseball cap and gave Bob Chin a slap on the back. Bob punched Matt in the arm. Matt was still rubbing the sore spot on his arm when Julio began doing a crazy dance. A roar went up as Matt, Bob, and Julio bolted out of the cafeteria.

"C'mon! Coach must have posted the roster," Michelle shouted. Her chair banged to the floor as she raced out of the cafeteria, not bothering to wait for Sandy or Skye.

Already the crowd in front of the bulletin board was at least ten deep. So what! Michelle bulldozed her way to

61

the front until her nose was practically flat against the glass. She went down the list with her finger.

"Yes!" she shouted, raising both arms in victory. "Sandy! Skye! I did it! I made it!"

But her smile quickly faded when she saw the sad expression on Skye's face. Something was horribly wrong. Puzzled, Michelle returned to the list. Keisha's name was there on the top line, but Skye's was nowhere to be found.

FINAL EAGLES ROSTER

Alevy, Derek	Kolumbo, Keisha
Cain, Kevin	Peterson, Matt
Chin, Bob	Rodrequez, Julio
Dupree, Michelle	Treschrizet, Abdul
Farrentino, Rocco	Wunderlich, Ed
Hardesty, Steve	

First practice begins Tuesday promptly at 3:30 P.M. in the gym. No excuses. Be there!!!!
                    Coach Hawkins

Slowly, Michelle threaded her way through the crowd to where Skye and Sandy were waiting.

"Oh, Skye, I'm sorry. Really."

"It isn't so bad," Sandy said, trying to cheer Skye. "Think of it this way—while Michelle is on the court playing, you and I can be in the stands with the Pep Squad and making tons of friends."

"It's no big deal." Skye's voice sounded sort of squeaky.

"I told you guys a million times, I never expected to make the team. Height isn't everything."

"You got that right," Derek boomed out of nowhere. He poked Matt in the ribs. "Not if you consider that the Eagles got stuck with two girls, and one of them's just a Smidge."

"Yuck, and she's a smelly tomboy, too!" Stephanie delicately pinched her nose.

"Butt out, Miss Cheerleader!" Michelle shouted, while glaring at Derek.

"Squash it, everyone," Matt said angrily, but it was too late. The damage had been done.

Michelle clenched her fists. She hated to admit it even to herself, but for once Bigmouth Brian was right. Just because the Coach made her and Keisha part of the team didn't mean all the guys had to accept them.

The next morning, for the first time since school started, Michelle beat Brian to the bathroom. She shampooed her hair with Sandy's orange-blossom shampoo and braided it while it was still wet. She used some of Brian's gel on her bangs. Afterward, she stood in front of the bathroom sink and stared at herself in the mirror.

Tomboy, huh. She'd show them.

"What are you doing in there?" Brian banged on the door. "Hurry up."

"I'm going as fast as I can."

Michelle opened the medicine cabinet and coolly inventoried the assortment of barrettes, tubes, bottles, and cans before grabbing the dark green aerosol.

Smelly, huh. Nobody was going to accuse her of having stinky pits.

Tough Guy, the label said in rugged white letters. *More powerful than any of our competitors.*

The television commercials showed handsome male athletes. "When you play your roughest, you need the toughest—Tough Guy."

Roughest, toughest—that was her all right. She couldn't chance smelling like an onion sandwich. Michelle snapped the cap off the can and gave each pit a quick *pffffffffffffttttttttt.*

"Hey, Bigmouth! It's all yours!" Michelle scooted back to her room to finish getting dressed.

Last night she had packed and repacked her sports bag at least a half dozen times. Now, just to be sure, Michelle checked it again. Socks, shoes, shorts, shirt, and towel.

With her bedroom door safely closed so no one could see, Michelle snapped her stupid slingshot sports bra in place and danced wildly around the room. She could hardly stand feeling so giddy inside. She was a firecracker waiting to be lit. Somehow she had to stay in control, get through her classes, and be ready to explode at her first Eagles practice.

Yes!

When the bell finally rang for dismissal, Michelle hurried for her locker. She crammed her books inside and yanked out her sports bag, slammed her locker shut, and gave the combination lock a quick turn. Then she slung the bag over her shoulder and headed for the girls' room to change.

A few minutes later, Michelle barreled through the gymnasium's double doors. She was no dink kid anymore. She was an Eagle, ready to fly. She barely noticed when some of the guys turned and stared coldly as she dropped her bag next to Keisha's.

"Yo, Short Stuff!" Keisha lobbed an orange blur.

Michelle caught the ball. Without bothering to think, she pulled herself into position and began dribbling down the court, past some boys, and toward Keisha.

They both knew the drill. Two bounces and a pass. Two bounces and a pass. When Keisha was under the basket, she leaped and shot. The ball tapped against the backboard and dropped smoothly through the net.

"Perfect!" Michelle snatched the ball.

TWEET!

"Bleachers, everybody," Coach bellowed.

Everyone scrambled. Five seconds later, Coach stood in front of them, legs apart, his whistle dangling on the silver chain around his neck. As soon as they settled, he began.

"Congratulations, Eagles!"

Chills ran up and down Michelle's spine as Coach scanned the bunch of them, then paused to gaze directly at her. She leaned forward, hanging on everything he was about to say, knowing that Keisha and the rest of them were doing the same.

"You are a fine, fine *team*." He boomed the word *team*. "I'll expect the best from you. That means showing

65

up on time, working together, and practicing seriously and with good sportsmanship. Got that?"

"Yes, sir!" everyone shouted together.

"Good! Then let's hustle up and move, move, MOVE!" He pulled five yellow pinnies out of a plastic crate. "Yellow team," he shouted. "Rocco, Kevin, Derek, Michelle, Keisha. Put these on and listen up for your positions. The rest of you work on your foul shots and layups. We'll switch over in exactly twenty minutes."

By four-thirty, Keisha was still going strong while Michelle was dead on her feet. By five o'clock, Michelle was ready for a coffin. But she'd never felt so good about a practice. Or a team.

"That's it for today," Coach shouted. "Good job. Remember practice is the same time, same place, every day—except Friday. No practice on Fridays. Got that?"

"Yes, sir!"

Michelle pushed her sweaty bangs off her forehead. Her legs felt like wet noodles. All she wanted to do was collapse, but now all the boys were heading out the side door with Coach. He was nodding his head at whatever Steve was saying to him.

Quickly, Michelle scrambled after them.

"Hey, wait for me, you guys!" She caught the back of Kevin's shirt. Stupid move.

Kevin whirled. "Wait? You can't go with us."

"Why not? I'm part of the team."

Kevin's laugh echoed in the hollow gym. "Hey, guys, don't hit the shower yet. We've got Smidge here trying to crash our locker room!"

Locker room? Michelle cringed with embarrassment. Not again!

"Hey, Short Stuff!" Keisha belted from the bleachers. "Don't leave me out here by myself. Is this your bag?"

Michelle slowly wandered over to sit down.

"Whew! That was some practice," Keisha said, rapidly unlacing her high tops. "You were smoking out there—running around like your pants were on fire."

Michelle unzipped her bag. "That Kevin is a royal pain. How am I supposed to know where the boys' locker room is? It's not like there's a sign or anything. Why is it always our fault when we don't automatically know everything?"

Keisha tilted her head toward another identical door. "Our locker room is through there. Not that it matters, since the custodian already locked it." She stood up to pull on her warm-ups. "So how long have you been playing, anyway?"

"Ever since my uncle sent my big brother a basketball for his fifth birthday." Michelle smiled. "What about you?"

Keisha twirled a ball on her finger like a globe. "I learned playing pickup with the boys. Then my dad took me to a pro game. It blew my mind! I joined the girls' league and here I am."

Michelle noticed that Keisha's eyes never left the ball. "I heard you played on the Eagles girls' team last year."

"Oh, please! Those girls spent more time getting their shorts pressed than they did shooting baskets."

Michelle chuckled before changing the subject. "So, are you going to the football game Friday night?"

Keisha gave the ball another spin and let it drop. "As far as I'm concerned, there is only *one* game and that's basketball." Keisha zipped-up her sports bag and slung it over her shoulder.

Wow! Talk about dedication. Michelle savored The Awesome Keisha for a few seconds. Should she ask for an autograph now or wait a few years?

"Let me know if you change your mind," Michelle said finally. "I'm meeting Skye and a couple of other kids. If you don't mind being seen with lowly sixth graders, you can sit with us."

Keisha's grin lit up the darkened gymnasium. "Thanks, but don't hold my seat. I've got some other stuff going on."

Michelle frowned. Keisha had come to the last game. Why couldn't she come to this one? Jefferson was pushing for its first win. What could Keisha possibly have planned that was more important?

CHAPTER 8

Luckily for Michelle, Coach didn't hold a Friday practice. As it was, Friday afternoon she had to rush around like an ant in a candy factory trying to get ready for the Eagles-Atoms football game.

At first it felt kind of weird when Sandy said she had invited another girl from the Pep Squad to sit with them. It had always been just Michelle and Sandy. But lately Michelle had been so busy with basketball that, except for catching the morning bus and a couple of minutes in homeroom and at lunch, she hardly ever saw Sandy. Besides, Michelle figured, she had invited Skye. Anyway, making new friends and finding different interests was what junior high was supposed to be all about.

"The Pep Squad is selling hair ribbons. You want to buy one?" Sandy held a curly blue and gold ribbon up to Michelle's face.

"Nah, I'd rather buy a soft drink at half time."

The field lights snapped on. Then the scoreboard. A hum of anticipation rushed through the stands as the Jefferson cheerleaders stretched a paper banner for the

Eagles players to break through. The drumroll sounded.

"GO, TEAM!"

The Eagles were pumped for a win. Brian had beefed himself up all week on pizza, pork and beans, and chili with nacho cheese, onions, and jalapeño peppers. Now, as everyone stood up and cheered at the teams running across the field, Michelle felt genuine sympathy for the Atoms. Brian was ready to blow.

As it turned out, when the girls started toward the snack bar at half time, the Eagles were down by fourteen points.

"Did you see the coach hollering at our guys?" Skye asked as they took their place in line.

Michelle glanced around, wondering if Keisha would show up. Meanwhile Sandy's friend, Roxanne, tried flirting with a group of eighth-grade boys who kept on walking.

"I don't blame him," Sandy said. "They really stink tonight. Oops! Sorry, Michelle. I didn't mean *all* the players. Brian is doing pretty good."

"Who's Brian?" Roxanne zoomed right in.

"My brother. The big loaf of bread with number 72 on his back," Michelle answered.

"And he is positively darling." Sandy batted her truly incredible eyes. "The biggest hunk in eighth grade."

"Maybe you could introduce us sometime."

Roxanne was begging to meet dork-brain Brian? Too stunned for words, Michelle paid for her soft drink and, shaking her head in absolute amazement, walked back to the bleachers with Skye.

There was no time to sit down. Half the town rose to its feet and roared as the Eagles prepared to kick off.

Oh, no! Michelle could hardly believe it. The Eagles only managed to kick the ball fifteen yards. Loose ball! The hulking Atoms surged for the ball. So did the Eagles.

Crack! Crunch! Michelle could hear helmets and shoulder pads collide even from where she stood. Whistles blew from every direction.

"Did we get the ball?" Sandy asked, joining them.

Michelle struggled to see over the person in front of her. "I can't tell."

"Well, do you *think* we got the ball?"

Skye, taller than anyone, craned her neck and squinted, her hand over her eyes like a visor. Michelle couldn't stand the frustration any longer. She held onto Skye's shoulders and climbed up onto her seat.

What a lousy mess. Practically every player on both teams had thrown himself into a heap in the middle of the field.

Why did guys do that? Did they learn The Human Haystack in practice? Once the ball was buried, she would have thought they'd stop piling on.

Michelle watched as the referees peeled the boys off the pile. So far, none of them wore Brian's blue and gold 72 jersey.

"Somebody's hurt," a grownup behind them gasped.

Michelle bit her lip. More players left the pile, but no 72. Finally only two players, both Jefferson Eagles, were left lying on the grass. Coaches and trainers from both schools crouched over the boys. The crowd grew quiet as

71

an ambulance inched its way onto the field. A sob caught in Michelle's throat. One of the players was Brian.

And then the big lug stood up and started bouncing around on his feet. He turned around, took off his helmet, and bowed to the crowd.

The applause wasn't exactly deafening. Everyone was busy watching medics lift the other player onto a stretcher.

Sandy turned to the grownup behind them. "Who is it?" she asked.

"Number 11, Kevin Cain."

Michelle arched her eyebrow knowingly at Skye. "If he's hurt badly, there's an opening on the basketball team. I wonder who'll tell Coach."

"Your coach is already here," Roxanne piped up. "I saw him at the snack bar."

A few minutes later the announcement came over the PA system. "Ladies, gentlemen, and students. We've had a serious injury on the last play. Kevin Cain, Number 11 for the Jefferson Eagles, will be replaced by Number 15, Chris Lambrosky. The Eagles would like to dedicate the remainder of the game to Kevin with the hope that he has a speedy recovery."

An earsplitting cheer sounded for Kevin.

Unfortunately, it didn't help the Eagles. They still lost big. But Michelle thought what happened next was even worse.

When the final whistle blew, with everyone from both schools watching—including Coach Hawkins—Derek slammed his helmet to the ground in utter disgust.

It didn't take a psychic to read Derek's mind.

If the football season was lousy, basketball promised to be even worse, especially now with girls on the team—one of them more a Smidge than an Eagle.

Monday morning, Mrs. Walbrecker, the girls' homeroom teacher, had a note waiting for Skye on her desk. Without saying a word, Skye gathered her books and left the room.

Michelle glanced at Sandy, who shrugged.

"So, guess who Coach picked to replace Kevin on the team?" Skye proudly announced when they finally met in the lunchroom.

Michelle whooped. "Yes!" Immediately, she began jumping up and down and hugging Skye around the waist.

"Great! Now the Eagles have the shortest kid, the tallest kid, and the coolest kid on the same team. Wow! Wait till Keisha finds out! When do you start?"

"This afternoon." Skye grinned. "I already called my mom. By now she's probably in the mall buying me more muscle bombs."

"It's muscle *balm*, silly!" Michelle giggled. "Unless you want your muscles to positively explode."

Skye gasped. "Never. Not in a million . . ."

"I don't believe it," Sandy moaned. "One Eagle girlfriend was bad enough. Now I have to put up with two of you!"

Skye gave Sandy a worried expression and Sandy burst out laughing. "Skye, I was only teasing! Congratulations!"

That afternoon, they got their first taste of Coach's temper. "I'd like to talk about the horrendous tantrum we had the displeasure of witnessing after Friday night's football game," Coach began.

Michelle's heart all but stopped when he gave Derek a long hard stare. "It had better never happen on the basketball court."

"Don't worry, Coach," someone quipped, trying to cut the tension—or rescue what little remained of Derek's pride. "We don't wear helmets."

"With heads that big, how do you expect a helmet to fit?" Keisha retorted.

Coach eyed Keisha. His jaw muscle flexed, but he didn't say a word. When Keisha didn't break his gaze, he turned back to his clipboard and took a deep breath.

"Listen up, now." He paced in front of them. "As a result of his broken leg, Kevin will not be playing football—or basketball—the remainder of the year." He paused, allowing what he said to sink in before nodding in Skye's direction. "Taking Kevin's place on our team is Skye Davidson."

Michelle noticed the guys in front of her snickering and bumping shoulders. Just what they needed—another girl.

Coach's jaw muscle tensed. He pinched his lower lip and stared hard at the offenders until they froze in place.

"Matt! Keisha! Bring that box in from my office."

A few minutes later, Matt and Keisha were ripping the tape off the box.

"Yo! Team jerseys! Reversible!" Keisha shouted, holding up a jersey for all to see.

Suddenly, it was Christmas. Minor annoyances disappeared as the team stood in line waiting for their jerseys.

"Listen up! Our Downtown Business Association generously donated these jerseys. Now I want your size!" Coach blared.

"Large."

Coach dropped a blue jersey in Abdul's hands.

"Next."

"Extra large."

"Next."

"Large."

"Next."

"Smidge," Michelle shouted.

Everyone cracked up, including Coach.

"Is that small?"

"Yes, sir."

Skye was next. "Stretch!" she shouted, bringing the whole place down.

The girls didn't wait for the box to empty. Waving their jerseys like flags, they sprinted for the girls' room.

"Blue side out," Coach shouted behind them.

"Yes, sir!"

In the girls' room, Michelle stripped off her T-shirt. She could hardly believe this was happening to her, and having Skye to share it with made it even better. The jersey slipped on like a new smooth skin. Michelle paused in front of the mirror, turning to see herself from the back. "Eagles" was spelled out in big gold letters across her shoulder blades. Underneath was a big 78.

Wow! Skye's grin stretched as wide as she stood tall.

"You ladies going to gawk at yourselves all day?" Keisha held the door open. "Can't you hear Coach? Hustle up! Let's go!"

Three Eagles soared through the empty school hall. Three Eagles rounded the corner. Three Eagles entered the gym, ready to show the guys their stuff.

Then Michelle spotted Stephanie and stopped dead in her tracks. "Why do the cheerleaders have to be here today of all days? That stupid Stephanie bouncing all over the place makes me want to puke."

Keisha made a clucking noise with her tongue. "Then you better take your pink medicine, girl. Remember, those cheerleaders are gonna be in here almost every afternoon."

The cheerleaders, Stephanie in the lead, strutted along the sidelines, passing Coach and the rest of the team. Coach, busy showing Rocco and Matt a new play, didn't appear to notice.

You couldn't say the same for the rest of the team.

"Somebody ought to find her a busy intersection," Michelle mumbled.

Keisha hooted. "Yo, Smidge. You better cage that green monster."

Michelle blew a blast of air over her upper lip to cool her face. She scooped up the first loose ball she found near the bleachers. She ran along the center line, then cut across to the key to drive the ball into the nearest basket. *Broing!* It bounced hard against the rim.

Coach caught it.

He held the ball a long second before offering it to Michelle. That was when she noticed she'd sliced a path through his play.

Gulp. "Sorry, Coach."

The next time the whistle blew, Michelle tingled with

anticipation. She rubbed her hands together and dried them on her new shorts. Did the others want to scrimmage as much as she did? Wearing team jerseys, they looked like real pros.

"Skye," Coach said, referring to his clipboard. "Watch the plays so you can learn them. The rest of you, listen up."

He called out names. Derek, Rocco, Bob, Ed, and Abdul were in gold. Michelle, Keisha, Steve, Julio, and Matt were in blue.

"Yes!"

Startled, Coach looked up and smiled as Michelle scrunched her head into her shoulders. Apparently, Brian wasn't the only bigmouth in her family. She hadn't meant to yell out loud.

Feeling nervous, Michelle assumed her position on the court with the lanky Abdul guarding her. Derek took the ball to center. He passed to Abdul and cut around, heading toward the basket. Abdul pivoted, dribbled twice with Michelle hanging on like a fly, and quickly passed up court to Rocco. Steve guarded Rocco but not well enough. Rocco lobbed the ball to Derek who, even with The Awesome Keisha hot on his tail, managed to bring it in under the basket.

It would have been an easy two points except for Keisha. She blocked Derek, leaving him no place to go—or even breathe. He put the ball up for an overhead pass, and she was there. He brought the ball down, and her arms waved like brown windmills. Before Michelle could stop him, Abdul cut loose. He bolted around Derek, taking a fast handoff, then rose into the air with the ball.

The ball missed the basket. Like an octopus, Abdul was all over the place. So was Michelle. The ball came down with Abdul's long arms going up to meet it. It tapped off Abdul's fingers. Michelle grabbed it and in a split second worked herself free. Before anyone noticed, she was gone.

She never looked back. Eyes intent on her goal, Michelle pushed the ball into the air. Almost in slow motion, it arced, falling with the barest *swish* through the net. Michelle blinked. If she'd been at home tossing socks through the toy hoop on her bedroom door, it couldn't have been any easier.

Derek's hand resting on her head brought Michelle back.

For a fraction of a second, his fantastically blue eyes twinkled like nothing else ever could. His whole face lit up with a smile he shared with her alone. "Nice play, Smidge."

A candy bar would have melted on the spot. In the next moment, Stephanie sauntered past with the rest of the cheerleaders. She'd seen everything.

TWEET!

"Switch colors!"

While Michelle and Skye stood, completely dumbstruck, the guys stripped off their shirts and turned them inside out.

"Smidge! Skye!" Keisha hollered from the doorway.

Of course. Why didn't she think of it before? They were girls! They had to go to the girls' room to change their shirts.

"Why can't we switch sides without reversing jerseys? What's the big deal?" she asked Keisha.

"The big deal is we wear either blue or gold depending on whether we play at home or away," Keisha replied, suddenly serious. "You've got to get used to both colors."

Michelle heard someone coming and groaned. She'd recognize that snooty laughter anywhere.

Stephanie was ready to sharpen her claws—on Smidge. "Jeez, would you look at those tacky shirts and shorts," she said to the entire squad of cheerleaders. "I mean, I wouldn't be caught dead in them. I'd much rather wear . . ." She gave a spin to set her blue and gold pleats whirling. ". . . something smart like this."

"Well, don't worry," Michelle piped up. "You couldn't fit in one of these shirts if your life depended on it."

Stephanie sized Michelle up and down, which didn't take long. "You're probably going to be the only girls in the district playing with the guys. You're not cool. You're freaks."

"Hustle up!" Keisha said under her breath. And out loud, "Takes one to know one, Teacup."

Quickly, they darted into stalls. Michelle stripped her jersey off and back on again.

"No other girls? What if that's true?" Michelle said as they returned to practice.

Skye shrugged. "Who knows?"

Keisha kept walking. "Who cares?"

CHAPTER 9

For Michelle, each practice so far had been an Olympic experience. Even the routine drills challenged her beyond all expectations. Coach treated each team member with equal respect and demanded hard work in return. He kept them alert and on their toes.

Today, standing on the sidelines, he fired a basketball at each of them as they entered the gym.

"Steve!" *Thwap!* "Jump shots!"

"Yes, sir!" Steve took off at a run.

"Derek!" *Thwap!* "Set shots."

"Yes, sir!" Derek followed Steve's lead.

"Skye!" *Thwap!* "Foul shots."

Glancing backward at Michelle, Skye dribbled slowly toward a far basket.

"Can't hear you," Coach shouted after her.

"Yes, sir!"

"Michelle!" *Thwap!* "Left-hand layups."

"Yes, sir!"

There wasn't a better feel than the ball's tight texture hitting her fingers or a better sound than the basketball's hard, smacking bounce. While the slanted rays of afternoon sun fell in a lazy puddle in the middle of the gym, Michelle and her teammates began another practice.

Skye shot a ball from the foul line and trotted in for the rebound. Standing in the key, Matt took a shot. *Swish.* Michelle steadily dribbled in a zigzag course from the left, driving toward the basket.

Here I come, the female Michael Jordan, zig to the left, zag to the right, the best girl player in the entire junior high conference, about to score the winning basket. Best girl, me? How do I know that? There's got to be other girls playing . . .

As quickly as her mind veered off course, so did the ball. It hit her toe instead of the floor, bounced out the door, and sailed into the hallway. Michelle zoomed after it. Maybe if Coach noticed her hustle, he'd overlook her inexcusably simple beginner's mistake.

Whoa! Two arms reached out and grabbed Michelle by the shoulders just as she was about to crash into a man wearing a rumpled plaid shirt.

"Hey, Shorty, watch where you're running!"

"Sorry." The ball ricocheted off the wall beside the water fountain and rolled back toward her.

"So are the junior high kids still here? I'm looking for the basketball team."

Michelle scooped up the ball and pointed with her thumb. "We're in the gym."

"Thanks." He pushed his cap back on his head to get a

better look at her. A camera hung around his neck on a leather strap. "You must be the mascot. Don't worry. I'll be sure to get you in the picture."

Michelle stiffened. She raked her bangs into stiff blonde spikes. "I am *not* the mascot. I'm an Eagle. I'm very much on the team."

The man shook his head in disbelief as he walked with her toward the gymnasium. "Boy, you'd think I'd remember by now that this year some of our junior high teams have girls on them."

A slow, quiet smile crept across Michelle's face. "Do you take pictures of all the teams in the district?"

"Yep. And your school's the last in the bunch."

Michelle shifted the ball to her other hip and cocked her head. "It is? So, which schools have girls on their teams?"

"Not too many, actually." He scratched his cheek. "Roosevelt, Barrett, and one other team I can't remember. You'll see the pictures next week in the *Journal*. We're doing a big issue just in time for your quarter break next week. It'll come out on . . . Wow, are you tall." He stopped abruptly when Skye stepped in front of him. "I bet I know why you're on the team."

Skye blushed and hugged a basketball to her chest. If she could have scrunched behind Michelle, she would have.

"This guy's a photographer." Michelle wondered if he even suspected that he'd given her vital information. "He's taking our picture for the paper. Right?"

"That's the tall and short of it." He laughed awkwardly at his own joke.

"You're late," Coach boomed as they entered the gym.

He strode over in their direction.

"Yeah. Traffic was lousy. You want to take the shots in here?" The photographer glanced around, noting the large windows, the bright fluorescent lights.

Coach didn't have to bother with his whistle. Seeing the photographer, the rest of the team naturally wandered over. So did Stephanie and the cheerleaders, who didn't exactly get in Coach's face, but stood close enough to scope everything out while the photographer fiddled with his lenses.

"We'll want to see everybody so let's put the short kids in front, tall in the back." He gestured to Michelle. "Little buddy, you can get in the middle. Just hold the ball like you're doing now." He nodded. "Good."

Michelle wished Coach would turn around and catch Big Shot Stephanie throwing kisses to the guys.

"They're not getting their pictures taken like *that*, are they?" a cheerleader whispered loudly. "They're all so grungy and gross."

"Oooh, their shirts are all sweaty and everything."

Nobody had to guess whose voice that was. Derek turned on his heel and started to leave.

"Hey, Coach, we'll be right back."

"Where are you going?" When Coach grabbed Derek by the arm, Derek turned about a million shades of red.

"Uh, we gotta . . . you know . . . do something about our hair and stuff. We don't want our pictures looking like this."

Coach made a face. "What is this? Why don't you freshen your makeup while you're at it?"

Poor Rocco. Taking Coach at his word, he started for

the locker room. Michelle smothered a giggle.

"Get over here, Sweet Cheeks. Let the man take a picture of a hard-working team for a change."

Michelle had to bite her lip to keep from laughing.

"Okay, Coach Hawkins." The photographer peered through his camera. "If you could move over by the foul line. That's it. I think I can get everyone in the shot."

While the rest of them waited for directions, Skye slid her ponytail holder out of her hair. She bent at the waist and shook out her long mane, then whipped her hair back over her shoulders. Steve, watching her, almost fell over.

"You, the model," the photographer called out when she was finished. "You stand beside Coach Hawkins."

He positioned Michelle, holding the ball, exactly in the middle of the front row between Matt and Bob. Keisha stood directly behind her. Michelle pressed her bangs into place and prepared to smile.

"Say, 'win-win-win!'"

"Win-win-win," they chanted.

"Say, 'play-play-play!'"

"Play-play-play," they shouted, cheerleaders included.

Red and purple lights exploded before Michelle's eyes.

"That's it. Thanks, guys. It'll be in next Tuesday's edition." The photographer waved his hat as he left.

TWEET!

"Listen *up!* Let's get back to business! You, pompoms." He turned to Stephanie and her crowd. "You get back to whatever it is you do best. We've got work to do here."

If Stephanie could have guessed what Coach was about to do, she would have figured out a way to hang around.

This time, Coach chose Derek for his demonstration.

"The other team throws the ball toward the basket." Coach held the ball in the air, but didn't throw. "Derek! What do you defensive players have to assume?"

"That it's going to miss?"

"Right." Coach handed the ball to Derek. "Okay, son. Now, let's say it's your shot and I'm guarding you. See?" Coach held his arms up to block Derek. "Now, what's my position?"

"Between me and the basket."

"Good answer." Coach nodded at Derek, who shot for the basket with Coach guarding.

"The moment the ball leaves his hands," Coach bellowed out to the rest of them, "pivot! Immediately face the basket and box out. You see how I'm crouched with my elbows and buttocks extended?"

"Yes, sir."

"I'm ready. At the same time, he has to go around all this space I've created to get his rebound."

Coach straightened. "We're going to set up drills now. One on one."

Michelle and Keisha boxed out, no problem. Considering that she'd never done it before, Skye caught on fairly quickly. But the guys . . . Michelle shuddered. They seemed okay against each other. It was only when . . .

TWEET!

"Michelle! Rocco!"

Michelle scrambled from where she'd been helping Skye. A few minutes later, she and Rocco stood three feet apart in front of Coach with everyone else watching. She knew why Coach was doing this. He wanted to see how she'd react to playing against a guy at least four times her size.

Rocco's real name was Richard. Behind his back, some of the kids called him The Incredible Bulk. Others called him simply The Rock.

Coach tossed the ball to Michelle. *Thwap!* She caught it. Rocco glared in her face, arms outstretched, a hulking monster.

Scared, but not about to admit it, Michelle closed her eyes, anticipating the worst. She threw for the basket without bothering to aim.

She expected Rocco to pivot, to throw his elbows, thick as hambones, in both directions. When she opened her eyes, she expected to find his butt right in her face. But it wasn't.

TWEET!

"What kind of tippy-toe move was that?" Coach blared at Rocco so loud the cheerleaders stopped in mid-cheer.

"Holy cow, Coach," Rocco pleaded. "I can't do that. Michelle is a . . . girl."

Michelle blinked, dumbfounded. She wished Rocco would tell that to Stephanie.

Coach turned on his heel, leaving Rocco to trot after him like a misbehaving puppy. "Coach!" Rocco pleaded anew. "You don't understand. We can't do that. They're *girls!*"

A dead silence settled over the gymnasium. Coach glared. Then, "Next!" he commanded. "Derek! Keisha!"

By now the cheerleaders had stopped altogether and snuck over to watch from the bleachers.

Thwap!

Coach shot the ball at Derek with Keisha guarding.

86

Derek gave the ball a cool toss as Keisha whirled, throwing her elbows out, pushing her butt at Derek, solid as a brick wall. Startled, Derek fell backward, hitting the floor with a boom.

"Coach! We can't. Rocco's right. These are *girls*," Derek wailed. When he looked up at the bleachers, Coach followed his gaze and all but exploded.

"You pompoms can disappear on the double." His eyes all but bugged out as he glared at Derek. "And as for you, I don't *know* that word *can't*. You got that?"

"Yes, sir."

"NEXT!"

Coach didn't let up. He made them do the drill over and over again. The guys whined, throwing their arms around and stamping their huge feet on the floor. Michelle began to worry. If the boy Eagles didn't hate the girl Eagles after this drill, it would be a major miracle.

That wasn't the only thing she worried about.

For the first time, she noticed Keisha running out of gas. Instead of filling her spare moments with hyperactive Globetrotter tricks, she stood silently watching, a towel draped over her shoulders, appearing for all the world like a tired, spent athlete.

TWEET!

"Hustle up!"

What was this? Instead of sitting on the bleachers like the rest of them, Keisha was lying down on her back. Why didn't Coach say something?

"Okay, Eagles," he said instead. "We have our first formal scrimmage tomorrow after school against the Ravens."

He might as well have dropped an atomic bomb.

"Already? Tomorrow?"

Coach nodded.

Michelle sat back and smiled. The Roosevelt Ravens. According to the photographer, Roosevelt had girls on their team. Of course, that didn't mean they'd actually play. She wondered if she would.

"I want all of you dressed by three-thirty," Coach continued, tapping his watch. "Be ready for me in the boys' locker room."

Michelle couldn't have heard that right.

"Got it?" Coach yelled. "Repeat."

"Three-thirty. Boys' locker room."

"No way! In the boys' locker room?" Michelle squeaked.

Coach took a long breath. He rubbed his finger thoughtfully along the space above his upper lip. "And where else do you expect me to give the team pep talk? Around the flagpole?"

For the first time that afternoon, the boys laughed.

Michelle ducked her head between her knees, trying to hide her embarrassment. Judging by the blast furnace on her face, she was blushing fire-engine red.

Keisha rolled her eyes. "Anything else, Coach?"

"Yes!" he boomed. "But you'll have to wait until tomorrow. I'm saving it for our pre-game talk. Three-thirty. Be there."

"Yes, sir!"

"Fine. Now get a good night's sleep. And remember— Eagles eat Ravens. Come hungry!"

CHAPTER 10

"Carbs." Brian hunched over his sickening mound of spaghetti and meatballs. "Didn't Coach tell you to load up on carbohydrates for energy?"

If Michelle watched him spin another fat forkful of spaghetti and shove it into his mouth, she'd puke. Obviously, no one else in her family felt the tension the way she did.

Her mother reached over and patted her hand. "He probably told her to get a good night's sleep. Right, Sweetie?"

"Actually, he told us to come hungry. Supposedly, Eagles eat Ravens."

"Sounds good. What time is this game anyway?" her father asked. "We'll have to close the store early."

"Dad, don't do that," Michelle said. "It's just a scrimmage. It won't even count on the team's win-loss record." Michelle slid back in her chair. "May I be excused?"

Who was she kidding? Michelle scraped her half-eaten dinner into the garbage disposal and wandered into the family room. Her performance tomorrow was crucial if she wanted to make first string. Besides, all the kids would be there—watching.

She plopped down on the couch and aimed the remote at the TV. "I got it," she hollered when the phone rang. "It's probably Skye wondering what we can eat since Coach told us to come hungry."

"Yo, Smidge! You scared?"

She almost dropped the receiver at the sound of Keisha's voice. She could swear she heard basketballs bouncing in the background. Michelle covered her other ear. "What did you say? I can hardly hear you. Where are you anyway? Are those basketballs?"

"Yeah. I'm at the Community Center, working out the kinks."

"Well, talk louder," Michelle shouted.

"D'ya realize what's happening?" Keisha yelled into the phone. "Tomorrow it's us on the Dream Team, head to head against the Ravens!" she shrieked.

Michelle's stomach did a horrendous flip-flop. "Thanks for reminding me."

"Aw, Smidge, you're going to do fine," Keisha reassured her. "You got what it takes. Whoa!" A whistle shrilled in the background. "Things are starting to happen here. Gotta go," she said abruptly.

Click!

Michelle stared at the receiver. Coming from Keisha, those words of encouragement really meant something.

Later, in bed, she pictured herself on the court going through the plays with the team. She saw herself rebounding alongside Abdul and taking chest passes from

Matt. She felt herself fly across the floor, heard the chatter, the pounding ball.

She could do it. She'd mesmerize everyone watching—except the Ravens, who would never see her coming.

Her whole body tingled. Man, was she wired!

Michelle rolled over on her side. When she couldn't sleep, she punched her pillow and rolled onto the other side. She tried counting from a thousand backward. Nine hundred eighty-seven . . . nine hundred twenty-six . . . eight hundred ninety-nine . . .

Tomorrow couldn't come soon enough.

"What's this Smidge stuff?" Sandy asked Michelle at lunch the next day. She handed Roxanne a quarter in exchange for a plastic bag of blue and gold confetti. "Oh, I get it," Sandy said as her friend left to sell confetti at another table. "That's the name Derek gave you. Pretty cute." She raised her eyebrows meaningfully at Skye. "Sounds like he likes her. I wonder if Stephanie knows."

Michelle's face heated up. Just then, Stephanie and a group of cheerleaders cartwheeled into the cafeteria. Some of the guys whistled as the girls formed a line in front of the tables.

Michelle nudged Sandy. Instead of watching the cheerleaders, Skye picked at her sandwich, a sad, sick look on her face.

"Wow!" Sandy rattled on, completely oblivious. "Big time! Everyone is staying for this game. I heard the Ravens are sending three busloads of fans."

Michelle winced and nodded again in Skye's direction. Skye had slumped even lower in her chair. Michelle wished Sandy would take the hint.

The cheerleaders started a clapping cheer. "Give me a T." Clap-clap. "Give me an E." Clap-clap.

Sandy yelled over the din. "The gym is going to be packed floor to ceiling."

Suddenly, Skye pushed herself away from the table. Holding her hand in front of her mouth, she bolted out of the cafeteria.

"Now look what you did!" Michelle hollered at Sandy. "It's her first game! How could you be so insensitive!"

Michelle grabbed her purse along with Skye's. She knew from personal experience where Skye was headed.

A few minutes later Skye came out of the stall, wiping her mouth with toilet paper. "I can't do it. For a million dollars, I can't do it."

"But Skye, I'm depending on you. When you start to play, you won't even notice the other people."

Skye whimpered. "But I don't even know where the boys' locker room is."

Michelle opened her purse. "Piece of cake. It's right here on Brian's map."

The rest of the afternoon, Michelle fought to concentrate in all her classes while she drew basketballs in her notebooks. When the bell rang for dismissal, she almost fell out of her chair.

Too nervous to talk, Keisha, Skye, and Michelle quickly changed into their uniforms. They pinned the gaping armholes closed and strode purposefully toward the boys' locker room.

"Okay?" Keisha shouted in warning while banging on the door.

Someone opened it and a basketball came flying in their direction. Keisha batted it away with one hand. "Cool it, you guys."

The boys sat on two benches with Coach standing between them. Coach indicated where the girls should sit. Michelle sat down quickly next to Matt and waited while Coach checked his clipboard.

"You know what to do out there, guys. We've been over everything at practice." He put the clipboard on top of the locker. "Today you are all Eagles. I want you to stand proud, as proud as the great bald eagle."

Coach whipped something out of his pocket. He pulled a rubber skullcap tight onto his head.

You could have heard a feather land on the floor as Coach's piercing eyes challenged them from under his new bald head. He cleared his throat.

"As proud as the great bald eagle," he repeated. Then he bent and dug deep in his sports bag.

"Here, these are only for the warm-up," he said solemnly. He handed each player a skullcap.

Suddenly, the boys' locker room buzzed with activity. Laughing, Michelle pulled her rubber skullcap over her head, watching Keisha in the mirror, who was busy watching Skye. With their skull caps on, she could hardly tell the boys from the girls.

Slowly, the laughter faded from the room. Each of

them knew the seriousness of what came next.

Coach motioned them to form a circle. He put his arm out, hand extended. Silently, the players bowed their bare skulls and put their hands on top of Coach's.

"Go, Eagles!" they shouted.

Raising their arms in victory, they ran into the gym. The crowd erupted with loud laughter and cheers of support.

A familiar hollow feeling she identified as pre-game jitters settled in Michelle's stomach as she ran behind Matt in their warm-up drills under the basket. At the other end of the court, the hotshot Ravens in their black and red uniforms showed off for their schoolmates. She quickly noted the three girl Ravens, then turned to the stands to locate Sandy and Brian. That was easy enough. They were both waving madly and cheering.

The referee blew a warning whistle. Two minutes till game time.

A flurry of loose balls smacked the backboards. A hush fell over the gymnasium as each team returned to their benches for final instructions.

Coach bent down on one knee in front of the Eagles. Michelle leaned forward, intent.

"Listen up! These players go in first." Coach read out the names. "I'll be moving the rest of you in and out fast. So, pay attention. Let's give it all we got."

The referee blew the whistle.

The crowd got on its feet. As Stephanie and the rest of the cheerleaders began shaking their pompoms, Derek, Keisha, Rocco, Steve, and Julio shot across the floor and took their positions along with five Ravens—one of them a girl.

Michelle held her breath as the referee tossed the ball in the air. The Raven center outjumped Derek and tapped the ball to another Raven, who went driving down the court for an easy basket.

Right away, Derek took the ball out, passed to Julio, who bounce passed to Steve, then back to Derek, who shot the ball. *Swish!*

A boy Raven came out, replaced by a girl Raven. They put the ball in play. Pass, pass. The Raven faked left and went right, driving in for another two points. Derek passed to Steve. Loose ball and out of bounds. Ravens' ball. Two more points on the scoreboard.

Coach tapped Michelle's shoulder. She ran to the officials' table to sign in and wait for a timeout. Before she knew what was happening, she was on the court.

Steve trotted toward the benches. "Go for it, Smidge."

Now Derek had the ball. Michelle sprinted up court, cut to the left and darted back, losing her Raven guard in the process. She was wide open!

Derek passed, but not to her. *Thwap!* A Raven girl flew between Derek and Julio, picking off the ball in the process. They got an easy two points as the ball sank through the net.

The score was 8-2, Ravens' favor.

Julio took the ball out of bounds and passed it to Derek, who wasn't going anywhere. Quickly, he lobbed it to Michelle. Back to Julio. Ravens were all over the place, but none of them was near Michelle. Julio saw. He bounced the ball under a Raven's arm, right into Michelle's hands. Quickly, she pivoted. Then, protecting the ball with her body, she dribbled in.

For a moment, she felt like the lone Eagle on top of a mountain. Nobody was within miles of her. She let the ball loose. It arced, tapped the backboard, and dropped in.

Down the court.

Michelle's Raven had the ball. She hung on him like a bug. He threw and, right away, she whirled, prepared for the rebound.

Box out! She crouched down and stuck her bottom and elbows out. Behind her, she heard the Raven guard step back, crashing into his teammate. With the two of them mopping up the floor, rebounding was a cinch for the Eagles. She passed to Derek, who dribbled back toward their basket. Another two points!

The next time her guy had the ball, she lunged for it.

"Jump ball!" The referee blew his whistle.

Michelle heard the titters in the stands as she took her place opposite the Raven in the center circle. What a joke! Maybe she came up to his kneecaps.

The referee tossed the ball. Michelle jumped, but the Raven never had to. Flat-footed, he tapped it to a Raven girl who was wide open and unchallenged by an Eagle. How did that happen?

Michelle didn't have time to sort it all out until Coach motioned her back to the bench. As she watched both teams at work, it suddenly became clear.

Ravens or Eagles, it didn't matter—whenever a girl had the ball, the guys backed off. They wouldn't try to steal. They wouldn't go after a jump shot. Just like at practice, when a girl shot a basket, the guys wouldn't box out. Their faces weren't red from exertion. The stupid clowns were blushing!

Michelle stared helplessly at the scoreboard. The Ravens led 20-8. The Raven girls had figured out that the Eagle guys played scared when it came to girls. And the Raven girls used that fear to good advantage.

The referee blew his whistle.

"Foul! In the act of shooting a basket. Two free shots."

Michelle held her breath as the referee handed the ball to Skye. She threw it over the backboard.

Michelle groaned. Skye's next ball didn't come anywhere near the basket. A bunch of smart alecks booed.

The Ravens took the ball out. Even from where she sat, Michelle could hear Keisha's chatter. Obviously the Raven point guard felt outmatched, trying to handle someone as awesome as Keisha.

Keisha crouched, arms wide, chatter still flowing. "Easy, baby. Easy, easy. Come on. Bring it down. Bring it down."

The Raven dribbled right, then left, and tried to pivot. But Keisha had him locked in tight and frustrated as she lured him in. Before he knew what was happening, she snatched the ball—a smooth steal you usually only saw with the pros.

"Go, Keisha!"

Keisha broke loose and flew down court, the ball banging beside her on the floor. Derek was waiting under the net and completely open.

"Keisha, here!"

Keisha heaved the ball—not to Derek, but to a Raven guard!

Michelle couldn't believe it. Anyone else might make a mistake like that, but not Keisha! The other Eagles were as stunned as she was. The Ravens scored without opposition.

Coach motioned a timeout.

Anyone could see the Eagles' fire was gone. When the game resumed, it seemed an eternity before the Eagles got the ball anywhere near the basket. Finally, a pass went inside the key to Keisha for a set shot.

The ball bounced off the rim and the buzzer sounded. Half time! Dripping with sweat, both teams headed for their locker rooms.

Derek ran a towel across the back of his neck. "Aw, Coach. It's bad enough we got girls on the team, but do you have to play 'em? Every time Keisha gets the ball, she makes a mistake. Skye can't hit the broad side of a barn and Smidge . . ." He paused. "Coach, if you ask me, she could do a lot better."

"Maybe we shouldn't throw them the ball," Rocco said under his breath.

"You stick your Eagle neck out like that, proud, bald, or not, you'll be off the team. They don't call me Hatchet-Face for nothing," Coach roared at Rocco. "You boys aren't thrilling to watch either. Now this is a team. You go back out there and hustle. And *think* while you're at it."

When the whistle blew for the second half, Michelle raced onto the court, determined to raise their score.

A few minutes later, a Raven girl put the ball up. It bounced off the backboard. Keisha, newly charged, went airborne. She rebounded and, in one fluid motion, landed, pivoted, and lobbed the ball to Derek as he tore down court wide open. Wow! What a throw! What a catch! What a play! Derek's hands took the ball on the run and dumped it in the basket.

Without thinking, Michelle patted Derek on the backside. "Nice job." Then she blushed.

She trotted back to the bench as Julio went in.

After that superb play, it looked like the Eagles might catch the Ravens. They struggled, bringing the score up to within five points. But then the Ravens put all three girls in at once. And, just as Michelle suspected they would, the Eagle boys choked.

When the final whistle blew, Michelle could only stare at the scoreboard in disbelief. Ravens 38. Eagles 22. The Ravens hurried over to shake hands.

Coach waved his arm, calling the team over for a quick conference before the stands completely emptied onto the court.

"Okay, everyone. We know what we have to work on. That's what a scrimmage is for."

All their faces showed the same dazed expression. If Coach was trying to make them feel better about losing, it wasn't working.

"It's your quarter break with two days off from school, but that doesn't mean two days off from practice," Coach went on. "I'll be out of town, but I want you in here at noon both days. Mr. Forsythe will be in my office if you need anything. I expect you to conduct yourself as Eagles," he said, gesturing with his fist, "and I'll see you on Monday."

Michelle pulled on her jacket, zipped it up, and started out of the gym along with Skye and Keisha. Directly in front of them, Derek turned, probably to find Stephanie.

"Derek!" Michelle started to say something about how they'd do better next Tuesday when they played the Barracudas in a real game. But as their eyes caught, he scowled and turned his back on her. Quickly, he threaded his way through the crowd.

He couldn't wait to get away.

CHAPTER 11

O utside, a faint autumn breeze rustled the leaves, sending them floating ever so peacefully to the ground. Inside, Michelle crept up the stairs, being careful to avoid the stair that creaked. With one hand, she gripped Hercules by the collar.

"Shhh, Herc! Quiet."

Hercules held his plumed tail high. He knew something was afoot as he sashayed beside Michelle toward Brian's room.

In Michelle's other hand, she clutched Hercules' greatest treasure—the only thing he adored more than tennis balls, the paper boy, or pizza. Michelle held Hercules' neon-green Frisbee.

Their parents had gone to work ages ago, leaving a note asking Michelle and Brian to walk to the grocery store. Problem was, Brian was still snoring in his bedroom, catching flies with his big fat mouth.

Not for long.

Michelle wedged the Frisbee under her arm so she could turn the doorknob. No doubt about it. Brian sawed some heavy logs. Someday she ought to make a video of him snoring. She could bring it to school as a science project.

She gave the door a gentle push. There he was, buried under a mound of crumpled sheets and blankets.

"Hercules! Fetch!" Michelle hollered at the top of her lungs.

Like he'd seen a ghost—or worse—Brian sat bolt upright. In the same second, Michelle gave the Frisbee an expert toss—right in Brian's lap.

Then she let go of Hercules' collar.

When Brian stumbled downstairs, barefoot, in his jeans, and still wrinkled from sleep, Michelle was noisily crunching cans for their recycling bin.

"Mom says we have to go to the store. You better get moving," she told him.

"Can't, Shrimp. Hercules mangled every bone in my body."

"Then how come you're walking, Morning Breath?"

"It's a miracle, but it won't last long. Only as far as the refrigerator." He pulled it open. "There's nothing in here."

"Duhhhhh. That's why we have to go to the store. Don't worry. You can inhale donuts on the way home."

He snarled.

"I don't know what your problem is," she said as she bagged the garbage. "It's because of you we have to go in the first place." She tossed the bulging bag at Brian. "Here, we have to get moving. Ditch this in the garage."

An hour later, Michelle wheeled a cart through the grocery checkout line. The sign said ten items or less, cash

102

only. The lady in front of her had seventeen items, not counting her umpteen rolls of toilet paper. Michelle groaned, seeing the lady fish around in her purse for a checkbook.

Clever Brian had skipped off to find something in the front of the store. Michelle glanced at her watch.

"Don't be late," Skye had told her over the phone. "My mother doesn't mind driving us to practice, but she gets real mad when she has to wait."

Good thing Mrs. Davidson wasn't in this line.

"Hey, Michelle," Brian said as she pocketed the change. "Why didn't you tell me you were growing a mustache?"

"What?"

Before she could stop him, Brian grabbed her by the sleeve and pulled her to the bulletin board. What was the big deal? Someone had tacked up a poster of Jefferson's basketball schedule. So? They did that every year.

Then she saw it. Somebody had taken a Magic Marker and painted black mustaches on all the girls' faces.

"Geez, do you think some little kid did it?" Michelle asked, afraid to think otherwise. "Maybe his mom gave him a set of markers for his birthday."

"Right. Get real, Michelle," Brian said sarcastically. "And his dad gave him a stepladder. Either that or he was a pretty big kid. How else could he reach this poster?"

Michelle shook her head, totally shocked. Vaguely she felt the bag of groceries slip out of her arms and into Brian's.

Who would do such a mean thing? And why?

It had to be someone who hated girls being on the

Eagles team. Someone who whined to the Coach when the girls didn't play like superstars. Someone who wanted to exclude girls from the plays and not pass them the ball.

What a fool she'd been to quit a winning all-girls' team to play with a bunch of conceited, whimpering boys. Here she thought she was doing so well for Jefferson by giving them her best, when apparently her best wasn't good enough. Some team.

Why didn't the boys get it? If she, Skye, and Keisha weren't the best players for the job, Coach wouldn't have picked them.

Oh, what was the use anyway? Hot tears rolled down her face. Suddenly, Brian reached out and ripped down the poster. He took her arm and, together, they stalked out of the store.

"Okay, you guys, listen up!" Derek announced once they finished their warm-up drills.

Keisha's nostrils flared. "Listen up? To him? Little Coach Peacock?"

TWEET!

"Give me a break, Derek."

Derek glared at Keisha. "Coach says we're supposed to do our regular routine. You missed warm-ups, Keisha. Think you can handle a five on five scrimmage?" Without waiting for an answer, Derek asked Matt to referee.

He handed Matt the whistle. "First team to fifteen wins."

Keisha jutted her chin. "Cool by me."

Skye stepped back, unsure. "So who are the teams?"

Matt held the pinnies. "Derek, Smidge, Rocco, Julio, and Keisha wear gold. The rest of you guys are blue."

When Matt blew the whistle, Derek jumped against Steve for the ball. Steve tapped to Bob, who bounce passed to Abdul. Michelle picked it off and quickly threw to Julio, expecting him to pass to Keisha as she cut around. Wrong. He passed to Derek.

Bad move! Angry that he'd lost the ball to Michelle, Abdul stuck his arm in and snagged the ball from Derek. He raced up the sidelines and plunked the ball in the basket.

"Hey, didn't you see I was open?" Keisha yelled to Derek.

"I saw." Derek took the ball out.

Michelle ran left, then cut right, losing Abdul in the process. She flashed in front of Derek, her hands wide and expecting the ball. Instead, the pass went to Rocco. He bounced it to Julio even though Skye had him covered like a glove. Meanwhile, both Keisha and Michelle were standing like two lost souls under the net.

Huh?

Michelle had never really expected Derek—or any of the guys, for that matter—to welcome her or any other girl onto the team. But she never expected to be shunned.

Before, even when they teased her about her height, Michelle felt like part of the team. Now with no teasing, no chatter, no recognition or passing the ball, she might as well not be here. The boys treated the girls as if they didn't exist.

Julio slipped the ball back to Rocco, who was about to lob the ball to Derek as he tore down court. Keisha saw the ball coming and sprang back to life. She flew between The Rock and Little Coach Peacock, arms raised, fists clenched. *Smack!* She batted the ball into the twilight zone.

"Hey!" Julio yelled.

"Yo, Smidge. Skye. You all do what you want. I'm not wasting any more breath trying to play ball with a bunch of buzzards. We get better practice on our own."

Head high, Keisha stalked off the court. She snatched a ball off the floor and moved methodically toward another basket. Michelle didn't wait for a second invitation. She thrust her shoulders back, stuck her nose in the air, and trotted off toward the equipment bags with Skye following meekly behind.

Michelle dipped into the canvas bag and handed a basketball to Skye. "They think they own the place. Let them try to scrimmage five on five without us."

"It'll be hard," Skye said. "There's only eight of them left."

Michelle was busy practicing layups when Matt wandered over. He glanced over his shoulder.

"Look, I don't really think it's your fault we lost the scrimmage game," he said in an undertone. "But the other guys don't want you on the team. It's that simple."

Michelle pushed her bangs off her forehead. "It's not that simple. We girls don't exactly appreciate the whole world seeing us wearing gross mustaches."

"Hey, it wasn't my idea. I tried to talk them out of it," Matt whispered back.

Out of the corner of her eye, she saw the hulking Rocco come toward them. Right away, Matt moved to the side to ponder a difficult shot.

Michelle turned to face Rocco.

He bounced the ball hard on the floor. *Boom. Boooom. Booooom.* Last bounce he caught with both hands. *Sssmmmack!*

Staring right at her, he faked a pass at her face, expecting her to flinch. When she didn't, he sneered and tossed the ball at the basket.

Ping! It bounced against the rim. And right into Michelle's hands.

Rather than tossing it up for a basket, Michelle threw the ball at Matt—hard—and stalked off. Boys! Even the nice ones were horrible.

That evening, Michelle didn't come down for supper. Instead, she stayed in bed and memorized her ceiling. Every once in a while, she haphazardly tossed a wad of trash toward the wastebasket.

Her mother tapped on her door. "May I come in?"

"Why not?" Michelle folded her hands across her chest. She crossed her feet at the ankles.

"So, how was practice?"

Michelle didn't answer. A lump lodged in her throat.

"That bad," her mother said. "Brian told me about the poster."

"Yeah." Michelle sniffed. "I always wanted a mustache. It goes with my tough guy, tomboy image." She shrugged. "It doesn't matter. I'm thinking I might quit."

"Michelle Marie!" Her mother only used her middle

name when she was ticked. "You're a member of a team. No quitting."

Michelle rolled her eyes in her mother's direction.

"What? A couple of weeks ago, you didn't want your daughter playing contact sports with a bunch of boys. Now all of a sudden, I *have* to? What gives?"

Her mother sat down on the bed. "I admit what happened hasn't been pleasant for you," she said. "You and the other girls will have to decide how to handle the situation. In the meantime, you haven't allowed yourself much time to relax since school started. You know what they say—all work and no play."

"I do play, Mom. Basketball, remember?"

"You know, Sweetie," her mother went on. "Dad and Brian are going camping over the weekend. You could ask some friends here for a sleepover. It's been a long time since you've done that."

"Mom," Michelle said crossly, "sleepovers are for babies. In junior high we pull all-nighters."

"Fine. That sounds even better. Set it up."

Michelle thought about it after her mother left the room. "Maybe I will."

CHAPTER 12

love all-nighters!" Sandy bounced the ball to Skye, who stood on the chalk line Michelle had drawn in the driveway. "Now, tell me again why Keisha couldn't come. She is so cool. I really wanted to get to know her."

"I did tell you, if you would just pay attention," Michelle snapped. "She said she had other plans. You can't expect someone like Keisha to want to spend the night with a bunch of sixth graders."

"Humph," Sandy said with a toss of her ponytail. "I think we're pretty neat."

Skye bounced the ball twice and prepared to throw.

"Bounce it one more time," Michelle directed.

"Why?"

"I don't know. I always bounce it three times. It brings me luck."

Skye bounced the ball again. She brought the ball up face-high and lined it up with the basket. "Okay if I throw it?"

"No. Just stand there all day."

"Geez!" Sandy shouted. "You are in such a rotten mood!"

"I am not."

"Yes, you are." Skye handed the ball to Michelle. "It's me, isn't it? Maybe I should just quit."

"Quit!" Michelle shrieked. "You can't quit. It's not you. It's those dumb boys. They acted even worse at today's practice. And Keisha . . . what is the matter with her? She's completely lost her zip. When Rocco Socco ran bellyaching to Coach at the last game, he wasn't exactly off the wall. Keisha made a ton of ridiculous mistakes, not to mention she looked dead on her feet."

"Maybe she had the flu," Skye suggested.

"I don't think so."

Sandy snapped her fingers in inspiration. "Maybe there's a conflict at her house."

"She'd never tell if there was."

"Darn," Sandy said. "It just kills me when I can't find out any juicy gossip."

"C'mon, Skye." Michelle passed her the ball and waited. "Bounce three times and shoot so we can go inside and order the pizza."

It dropped through the net first try.

"I'm impressed," Sandy said as she caught the ball. "If you keep it up, Skye, you're going to be the star player. Now what do you say? Let's get a pizza that's really loaded."

"Not too loaded. We don't want to get a stomachache," Skye cautioned as they entered the kitchen.

Michelle turned to Sandy. "I picked out a bunch of cool videos for after the game."

"What game?"

"Oh, I thought I told you." Michelle set the phone

book on the counter. "Mom's dropping us at the Community Center for the league game between the Rockets and the Hornets. It's going to be great."

"Not more b-ball." Sandy pretended to pout. "Oh, well. Maybe I'll meet a cute guy there. You never know."

Michelle swatted her with a dishtowel. "Are guys all you think about?"

On the way over in the car, Michelle's mother gave them their usual instructions. Stay together, and inside the Community Center. No talking to strangers. She'd pick them up at ten o'clock sharp. The girls rolled their eyes, but nobody really minded. Knowing that their mothers cared always made them feel good.

When they arrived at the Community Center, Michelle felt out of place searching for a spot in the stands instead of preparing to play. But scoping out the gym was even weirder. Had it shrunk? Or was Jefferson's gym absolutely gigantic by comparison?

They'd barely laid their jackets on their seats when Keisha trotted out in a Hornets uniform. The three girls gaped in surprise.

"What's she doing here?" Sandy asked.

"Playing, obviously," Michelle answered tartly. "I thought she quit the league when she made the Eagles. So that's why she couldn't come to Friday night's football game. I can't believe she didn't tell me."

Restless with what she'd discovered, Michelle tapped her foot on the bleachers in front of them until the man sitting there asked her to please stop. She couldn't help it. Why didn't Keisha tell her she was playing for two teams?

"Look." Michelle nudged Skye. "Keisha is in every play. The Hornets keep feeding her the ball."

Keisha took another pass.

"You're right," Skye said. "It doesn't even matter if she's open. They throw it to her anyway."

"This isn't basketball," Michelle said, disgusted. "It's a one-girl team."

"That's not all," Skye whispered. "The other kids are going in and out. Keisha isn't getting any rest."

"The league has games two nights a week and practice three nights. Keisha is playing basketball practically around the clock. No wonder she's tired. She's running her legs into the floor."

"Why would she want to do that?"

Michelle shrugged. "Beats me."

"So what are we going to do?" Sandy asked at half time. "Do we tell her we're here?"

Michelle nodded. "You guys go on to the snack bar. I'm going to ask her again to spend the night."

As soon as the others left, she scooted over to the bench where Keisha sat, head bent, a towel draped over her neck. "Yo, Keisha," she said softly.

Keisha jumped a mile.

"Some game." Michelle sat down beside her. "The Rockets don't know what hit 'em." She paused. "The invitation to spend the night still holds. We've got excellent junk food, videos, and you can crash in one of my dad's shirts if you want. Why don't you see if you can come?" Michelle nodded her head in Sandy and Skye's direction. "My mom's picking us up after the game."

Keisha smiled the same bright smile Michelle knew from practice. "Yeah. Sounds like fun."

"Good."

"Yo, Smidge."

Michelle turned.

"You're okay, you know that?" When Keisha held her hand up, Michelle hit it.

If it surprised her mother that they were bringing another kid home from the game, she didn't let on.

"Okay, girls," she said after they'd carried armloads of blankets and pillows into the family room. "I have to get to the store early tomorrow morning so try not to make too much noise. Be sure you remember about Hercules."

Keisha sat on the couch with a can of tennis balls. "What about Hercules?" She kept tossing the balls to Hercules, who kept wagging his tail and bringing them back.

"Oh, she just means we can't let Hercules get any of our food. The last time I had an all-nighter, Hercules went to the bathroom in the upstairs hallway. By the time my mother found out, it was too late."

"You should have heard her," Sandy said. "She went totally ballistic."

Keisha laughed. When she didn't toss the ball fast enough, Hercules barked. "He's a neat dog. We can't have pets in our apartment." She paused. "I wouldn't have time for one anyway."

Michelle saw her point. If she played basketball for two teams and had practice around the clock, plus school work, she wouldn't have time for a pet either. Michelle couldn't imagine not having Hercules.

"Well, if you ever want to play with him, come on over," she told Keisha. "You don't even have to ask."

Keisha yawned. "Thanks. I just might."

"I know!" Sandy said suddenly. "Let's do make-overs. I've got a bunch of magazines in Michelle's room. When my mom tells me to throw them out, I bring them over here. Right, Michelle?"

Michelle rolled her eyes. "We hide them in the crawl space," she told Skye.

Sandy folded an arm across her chest and placed a finger against her cheek. She looked at Skye very intently. "We really ought to do something about your hair."

Skye jerked backward, grabbing her long brown hair protectively. "What's the matter with my hair?"

Keisha yawned loudly. "You guys go upstairs. I'll dog-sit Hercules."

The other three girls weren't gone even five minutes, but when they came back, they found Keisha sound asleep on the floor with Hercules snuggled up beside her.

Sandy stood, her toes next to Keisha's nose, and waved her arms as though directing a chorus. She started to sing. "Every party has a pooper . . ."

"Shh." Skye grabbed her arm. "Leave her alone."

"I don't want to leave her alone. It's an all-nighter. Besides, I want to know what she was doing playing b-ball at the Community Center." Sandy turned to Michelle. "You didn't find out anything. I thought you were going to ask her. How can you let her go to sleep? Let's give her some of your mom's instant coffee before she totally zonks out."

Skye gazed at Keisha the way a doctor might. "How

can she go to sleep with big hairy Hercules sleeping on top of her? It's probably not even healthy."

"She's completely totaled. Even Brian doesn't pass out that fast." Michelle could have shouted into a megaphone and Keisha wouldn't have budged. It was pretty spooky.

Sandy shifted her weight to her other leg. "Is she breathing? Let's get a mirror. I've got one in my purse."

"I know what's happening," Skye said. "Her body is restoring itself. I wonder if she takes vitamins." She turned to Michelle. "Does your mother have orange juice for breakfast?"

Sandy started for the kitchen. "Yeah, her mother's got everything," she called over her shoulder. "Come on, let's forget about the mirror and warm up some leftover pizza. We can do make-overs after we eat."

"Nah," Michelle said, stepping over Keisha's exhausted body to follow Sandy into the kitchen. "Let's fix popcorn."

"Great! Let's have both. What about corn chips? Do you have corn chips?" Sandy opened a cabinet.

Skye made a sick face. "I don't think popcorn goes with pizza."

"We have chocolate," Michelle told Sandy. "Did I ever tell you how beloved Brian piles chocolate ice cream on top of cold pizza—for breakfast?"

"Oooh." Skye held onto her stomach. "You guys are making me sick."

"Why?" Sandy looked surprised. "We're not having that for breakfast. There won't be any pizza left."

Michelle stuck the pizza in the microwave and closed the door.

"Hey, let's try doing it together!" Sandy stuck a bag of microwave popcorn inside.

"You guys!" Skye shrieked. "I am not going to eat any of that!"

Michelle shrugged. She punched the numbers on the microwave and let it roar.

Wow! What a neat smell. Meanwhile, Sandy plunked ice and poured sodas into glasses. Then they carried everything into the family room and set it on the table in front of the couch. While Michelle stepped over Keisha to push the video into the VCR, Skye curled up on the couch with a pillow and blanket. Michelle glanced at Sandy. When Skye stretched her legs out, they took up all three cushions.

Oh, well. Michelle and Sandy sank down on the floor in their usual spot with their backs against the couch and the pizza and bowl of popcorn between them.

"Is it a scary movie?" Skye asked.

Sandy picked up the video box and pretended to read it. "Not really." She did a fake double take. "Michelle, did you really have to get a basketball movie, too?"

What was she talking about? Michelle lunged for the box but Sandy scooted away quicker than she could grab.

"It's about three girls who join a boys' basketball team," Sandy said, still pretending to read the box. "The boys retaliate with chain saws. It's rated VB for Very Bloody."

"Yeaaaach!" Skye leaned off the couch. "You guys are giving me pukey nightmares."

"Pukey? What kind of word is that? The next thing you know, she'll be saying things like *geeky*."

"Geeky. Geeky." Skye dissolved in a fit of giggles.

Skye sounded like a squeaky spring. Sandy must have thought so, too. She pounded the floor helplessly with her fist, she was laughing so hard. When Hercules started to bark, Skye got the hiccups. Michelle caught the giggles next.

Keisha never budged.

"I'm hungry," Sandy said, halfway through the movie. She and Michelle looked at Skye. She was asleep on the couch, and the movie hadn't even gotten to the good part. "Let's get those corn chips and take them upstairs."

"We've got salsa in the refrigerator."

"Great!" Sandy grabbed a bowl from the cabinet. "Do you have cheese? Let's get that, too."

Of course, they had to step over Keisha to get into the kitchen and back over her again to get upstairs. No problem. Keisha was out like Rip van Winkle.

Michelle and Sandy spent the rest of the night eating, babbling, giggling, and catching up on all the news they hadn't had time to share since beginning junior high. Michelle's mother was right; it was just what Michelle needed. Around four o'clock, they crept back downstairs.

An eerie light cast the room in empty shades of gray, and static crackled from the television set. Michelle snapped the set off as she passed it. Sleeping beside Keisha, Hercules woofed, chasing rabbits in his sleep.

Sandy flipped on the kitchen light. Outside the windows, it was still black.

"You want a donut for breakfast?" Michelle asked.

"Is it time for breakfast already?"

117

Michelle shrugged. "We ate all the pizza."

Sandy propped an elbow on the table and burped politely. "I can't believe we ate the whole thing. I'm going to lie down."

"Me, too."

"You guys really slept late." Skye poured Keisha a glass of orange juice. "I said good-bye to your mother for you. She put out what was left of the donuts for us. Keisha took care of Hercules. 'Yo, Dog,'" Skye mimicked. "'Do your thing.'"

Keisha grunted. "So? He went, didn't he?"

Too tired to care, Michelle yawned instead.

"Don't you want any breakfast?" Skye asked.

"Nah. We had ours already."

Sandy rested her chin on the table. "At four o'clock."

Skye blinked. "You were up at four o'clock?"

"Yeah. And three o'clock and two o'clock. We even put Herc out at one. Didn't you hear us?"

Sandy giggled. "It was funny. When Hercules came back inside, he crawled right over to Keisha and put his big head on her back. She never even budged!"

"When I sleep, I'm a rock."

Michelle nervously pushed donut crumbs toward the center of the table with her finger. She glanced at Keisha and went back to studying the crumbs. "So, Keisha, I need to ask you, how can you play for two teams?"

Keisha let out a long breath. "There's no conflict. They don't play against each other."

Michelle licked her finger thoughtfully. "That's not

what I meant. My folks wouldn't let me play on the league and for the Eagles with school and all. What about Coach? Does he know?"

Keisha shifted uncomfortably in her chair. "My parents are cool. Coach doesn't like it." Keisha made a face. "But he understands." She helped herself to the last donut. "It's important for me to play as much and as hard as possible. I have to be visible. Next year, I'll be in high school where competition is really tough. Coach says if you want a scholarship, you gotta work."

Michelle's hand dropped on the table. "You're working all right. They've got you in every play."

Keisha shrugged. "Can't be helped."

"I don't care what you say. It doesn't seem fair for you to carry that whole team. You could burn out."

Keisha balled a napkin in her fist. "I'm not burning out. I'm getting first-rate practice. According to Coach, that's what it takes."

"Well," Michelle sighed, "it's not good basketball when one person does everything. Basketball is teamwork. That's what Coach says. He also says we have to give a hundred percent. How can you do a good job when you're wearing yourself out like that? You play more ball than the pros."

"Not really, but, if it'll make you feel better, I'll talk to my league coach about giving the rest of the kids a chance to play."

"Promise?"

"Yeah, I promise." Keisha lobbed the napkin into the empty donut box. "Once I get used to the schedule, I'll be all right. I got a lotta good people behind me."

"Like who?"

"You. Coach. The rest of the team."

"Some team," Michelle said dryly. "The Eagles aren't a team. Not when you have boys who paint mustaches on girls' faces, don't throw to us in practice, and run like crybabies to Coach."

"Yeah!" Sandy said, suddenly waking up. "And then on the court they play like a bunch of wimps. Our guys are embarrassing."

"It's that obvious?" Michelle, Skye, and Keisha said at once.

"Personally, I think the boys are afraid of us," Michelle said. "I know at least one who's scared to death Keisha will show him up."

"I'm not going to play down to anyone. That's dumb," Keisha responded.

"They also think we're fragile," Michelle added.

"Jocks like you, fragile?" Sandy fluffed her hair with her fingers. "That's absurd. I'm the only one who's fragile. Look. My ends are always splitting."

The girls howled.

"Seriously," Michelle said, once the laughter subsided. "I have this crazy idea. Maybe we ought to re-educate the Eagles."

Keisha held two thumbs up. "Go for it, Smidge!"

CHAPTER 13

Michelle stood alone outside Coach's tiny office and stared in fascination as a rather round French chef on TV stirred a concoction with a long-handled spoon. Next he poured the liquid into a casserole dish and put it in an oven.

Michelle tapped the partially opened door.

Startled, Coach looked up from the video he was watching. "Michelle, what can I do for you?"

"I'm on my lunch period and I only have a few minutes, Coach. But I wanted to talk to you before our practice this afternoon."

Coach smiled, inviting her to tell him more. "Sounds important."

"Well, it is, kind of. It has to do with the wimpy way we scrimmaged. I don't think boys understand girls very much. To them, we're fragile."

Coach got up from his chair and came around to lean against the front of his desk. "And you're telling me that you're not. Does that go for the other girls on the squad?"

"Yes, and the girls on the other teams. They're not fragile either. I don't think the boys understand that. They don't box out. And if a girl has the ball, they won't try to steal it from her. They don't guard girl players the same way they do guys. And they don't want to throw to us because someone else might say that they like us or something. Coach, boys really play wimpy when there are girls on the court."

"Are you suggesting I tell them that?"

Michelle cringed. "No! We already know the boys don't want us on the team. If you call them wimps, they'll hate us even more. It might be a dumb idea, but maybe at practice you could have us bump around a little bit," Michelle suggested. "Then they could see that we won't break."

"I see your point," Coach mused. "Let me think a minute."

While Coach thought, Michelle stared at the television. The chef had disappeared. Now a team of waiters in white aprons carried his casserole, flaming, to a table.

"Attention," a heavily accented voice said in the background. "Voilà, la casserole!"

Michelle's mouth dropped. "Coach, that's it!" She pointed to the TV set. "Videotape us!"

Coach slapped his leg. "Why didn't I think of that? It's exactly what the pros do." Coach paused. "But they have someone to do the taping. I don't."

"You could ask my brother, Brian. He knows how to use a camcorder."

"Perfect! We'll make it a closed practice."

Michelle grinned. "That sounds great."

Coach nodded. "You run off and get some lunch. Oh, and Michelle . . ."

She stopped.

"It might be a good idea if we kept this conversation to ourselves for now."

"Sure, Coach."

TWEET! "Hustle!"

Everyone bolted for the bleachers.

"We're doing something a little different this afternoon," Coach began. "I've asked Brian to help us make a video."

Skye and Keisha had questions written all over their faces. Meanwhile, the boys flexed their pecs like movie stars. When Coach called their assignments, they swaggered onto the court.

"Hey, Brian. The camera, is it rolling? You catching my act?" Julio called.

"Brian, try to get a little bit of everything," Coach said. "Follow the ball with the camera."

Brian walked slowly along the sidelines. He peered through the viewfinder.

"Oh, and Brian," Coach said over his shoulder. "Don't forget to take the lens cap off."

Brian turned beet red. He put the cap in his pocket. "I knew that, Coach."

For the next fifteen minutes, the Eagles scrimmaged while Brian recorded everything on tape.

"Okay, guys!" Coach blew his whistle. "Thanks, Brian," he said, taking the tape. He held it in the air. "Let's see what we've got."

That was just what the boys wanted to hear. They strutted toward the media center and grabbed the chairs closest to the TV set. Coach slipped the tape in the machine and turned it on.

"Hey, there's Brian's big feet," someone shouted. "Pass the buttered popcorn."

Michelle leaned forward, trying to get a closer view of the screen. Wow! She moved faster than she ever imagined. But wait! The ball just whizzed past her. She remembered that happening. Now she saw why.

She flitted around like a gnat on a summer lake. No wonder she didn't get many long passes. She lost her guards with her abrupt turnarounds, but she lost her teammates, too. Half the time, she didn't stay in her pattern.

Michelle slid down in her chair with her shoulders hunched up around her ears. She never expected this.

Suddenly, Ed stood up and pointed to the screen. "Watch, you guys! Derek's gonna pass me the ball. Here comes a really smooth move."

Everybody groaned, Ed included. "So, I got picked off. Big deal. Nobody's perfect."

Coach stopped the tape. "Who's that in the corner?"

"Gee, Coach," Julio piped up. "It's difficult to tell. Maybe a bug landed on the TV set."

"That's Smidge." A bunch of boys laughed.

"She was wide open," Coach thundered. "If she got any closer to the basket, she'd be sitting in it." He pressed the button and the tape resumed.

"Geez, there's two points blown away because Bob muffed my throw," Derek moaned.

"Ready for another angle on that?" Coach asked.

Together they watched as Derek hurled a cannonball in Bob's direction that spun off his fingers, sending him out of play, injured.

Shocked, Derek turned to his teammate. "I could have really hurt you. I'm sorry."

"Forget it. Nothing broke."

"Hey, who's making all that noise?" Keisha asked.

Abdul gave Keisha a weird look. "What noise?"

"That . . . talking. There it is again."

"You mean, you?"

Keisha curled her lip. "That's not me."

"Atta boy, atta boy. Come to me, mama," Abdul imitated. "It *is* you. And when you don't have the ball, you're shouting for it. A real ball hog. Face it, Keisha, you're a machine. You never stop."

"A ball hog run out of gas," Derek said out of the corner of his mouth.

Michelle heard. "Since when is basketball about one person?" she said, coming to Keisha's defense.

"Smart," Keisha agreed. "That's exactly what I told my league coach."

Coach pressed the button and the action resumed. "Steve, what's happening there?"

"What do you mean? Skye's got the ball and I'm guarding her." Steve blushed. He easily could have grabbed the ball out of Skye's hands, but he didn't. "Coach, you can't go in after a ball when a girl's got it."

Michelle squeezed her eyes tight. That was exactly what she'd told Coach!

125

"Is that a consensus?"

Rocco scratched under his arm. "A what?"

"Is that opinion shared by the rest of the team?" Coach restated.

The boys mumbled to themselves.

The next play showed Michelle tossing the ball at the basket while Rocco guarded her. When he didn't box her out, she went in for the rebound.

"Anyone care to explain that?" Coach asked.

Michelle couldn't keep quiet any longer. "You guys think we're fragile because we're girls. But we're not."

"And we're not the only girls who know it," Keisha said, folding both arms across her chest.

"The Raven girls knew it," Skye added.

Keisha clucked her tongue in agreement. "Those Raven dudes didn't play mean ball with us either."

"We're not going to break," Michelle said.

Matt chuckled. "Not butting heads, you're not."

"See. Matt knows."

"Okay, so what?" Derek pushed back in his chair. "I mean, what do you expect? We're gentlemen."

"Gentlemen!" Michelle snapped. "Excuse me, but gentlemen don't paint mustaches on girls' faces."

"Cool it. It was only a picture."

"Get real, Derek. It wasn't your picture!"

Coach cleared his throat and everyone fell silent. "Okay, guys, what's done is done. Get past it."

The next part of the video showed Michelle throwing the ball to Abdul, who, even with his long octopus arms, had to reverse and run back up court to catch her wobbly pass.

"Good save," Michelle muttered. "Anyone else would have lost it."

Abdul shrugged. "S'okay."

Coach interrupted. "Next time, Michelle, try placing your hands more behind the ball with your fingers spread and your thumbs close together. You'll have more control. The same goes for all of you."

"Hey, look at Skye there under the basket," someone shouted. "She practically touches the rim."

Steve leaned toward Skye. "A little practice jumping and you'll be our first slam-dunker."

When Coach turned on the light, Skye was blushing.

"By the way, Michelle," Coach said. "Be sure to tell Brian that he did a great job. This is exactly what we needed."

Derek stood up. "So, are you going to keep the video?"

"Yes, sir," Coach replied. "And if you don't shape up, I'm going to leave it here in the media center for circulation."

Everyone groaned.

Matt raised his hand. "You wouldn't do that, Coach."

"Sure I would, Matt." He reached around to the librarian's desk for a marker. "How does 'Basketball Bloopers' sound?"

Coach tapped his fingers together. "One of our team members came to me today, thinking that, if we didn't make some pretty drastic changes in our tactics, we wouldn't win against the Barracudas. What this person said took a lot of guts. That makes me proud."

Derek and Rocco exchanged glances.

"I hope we agree that we have a lot to work on. Take a few minutes and think about what you saw on the video. I'm going back into the gym. We'll continue with our practice there."

Waving the video, Coach started for the door. "When you're ready to work, you can join me."

A hush fell over the library as the team played the tape over inside their heads. Matt was first to leave, followed by Bob. Ed left next, then Steve. Skye pushed her chair back and slipped out, then Julio, followed by Michelle, Keisha, and the others.

Stephanie met them in the hallway, a ferocious scowl pasted on her face. "You can't have a dance without inviting the cheerleaders."

What was she talking about?

Loud rock music came blasting at them from the gym.

Keisha barreled past Stephanie. "The sign says closed practice. If you get any nearer, you'll lose your earring in the doorjamb."

Coach waited until the team had all gathered around him before he turned down the volume on his boombox.

"What we have here is a do-or-die practice," he said. "Tomorrow we play the Barracudas, who have three outstanding girl athletes on their roster. Now we can either play like jocks, or we can play the way we did against the Ravens."

Coach rubbed his finger across his upper lip. "You do it on the dance floor. So now let's see some bumping in the gym."

Michelle's eyes almost popped out of her head. Her first junior high dance. And she didn't even have to buy a new dress or wear makeup. Wait till she told Sandy.

For the next fifteen minutes, the not-fragile girls banged shoulders against the boys. Hesitating at first, the boys hit back with their shoulders. Then the girls knocked the boys with their not-so-fragile hips. The boys closed their eyes. One by one, the girls got the boys to hit back.

Next, Coach set up drills to help the boys with boxing out. Finally, they worked on steals.

"We don't think about chests or behinds when we play," Michelle told the boys at the end of practice. "We think about putting the ball in the hoop."

She looked straight at Derek. "If you guys can do the same, we have a good chance of finally beating the Barracudas."

CHAPTER 14

G o, Eagles! Beat Barracudas! The Pep Squad pasted big blue and gold letters in the front hall, the cafeteria, and every wing of the school.

The hallways buzzed with excitement. Blue and gold crepe-paper streamers hung draped from the ceiling. Huge bows decorated every door. Even if Michelle wanted to, there was no ignoring the upcoming game.

Now that the shortened football season had ended, everyone's attention was riveted on basketball. Never before had Michelle known such excitement. Every pore on her whole body prickled with energy.

When she walked down the hallway, kids called out to her, "Good game today, Smidge!" She didn't even know some of the kids. She didn't know their names, but everyone knew hers.

Smidge. She held her head up high. If they'd called her Magic, it couldn't have sounded sweeter.

"Good luck today, Smidge. We're pulling for you. Get those Barracudas."

"Thanks!"

She turned down the hallway to take her books out of her locker.

Of course, stupid Stephanie had to be there waiting.

"Good luck today, Smidge," she said mockingly, making the new name sound like garbage.

Nothing and nobody, especially Miss Bounce for the Ounce, was going to ruin this day.

"Why, thanks, Stephanie. That's nice of you to say."

Stephanie glowered.

"I hope you know everyone's talking about your closed practice." She arched an eyebrow in a nasty way.

"Thank you." And then because Michelle couldn't resist it, "Have you seen Derek anywhere? I've got something for him." She stepped back, giving Stephanie a look of concern. "Gosh, Stephanie. You don't have to get so steamed. Save it for the game."

Michelle slammed her locker and snapped her lock shut before hurrying toward the cafeteria.

If Derek wanted a jealous monster like Stephanie for a girlfriend, he had a real problem. Stephanie didn't care if the Eagles won or lost. She only wanted to keep Derek all to herself and dangling on a leash.

Never mind them, Michelle thought to herself. She had other things to worry about now. Word of the team's exciting entrance as bald Eagles at the scrimmage against the Ravens had spread like wildfire. Kids who had never seen a game before became enthusiastic fans. Reporters from the *Journal* had special seats reserved in the bleachers. Funny, Michelle thought, how something as silly as skullcaps could make such an impact. After the yearbook staff heard how Brian had helped Coach with the video, they had even assigned him to take action photographs.

Michelle joined Sandy and Skye at their usual table in the lunchroom. Their conversation stopped when Matt bent over her shoulder and lifted a French fry off her tray.

"So, are you ready for the game?" he asked Michelle.

"Hope so. What about you?"

"I guess. A little nervous, maybe."

"Not me," Skye said, a sick grin on her face. "I'm a walking disaster."

"You'll do okay," Matt said sympathetically. "Just remember to bounce the ball a couple of times before you shoot those foul shots. Don't let the wait get to you."

Michelle smiled a silent thank-you at Matt, who nodded as if he understood.

"Um." Matt scratched the back of his neck self-consciously as he turned to Michelle. "What you did, going to Coach, took a lot of guts. We know it was you because of Brian making the video. I couldn't have done what you did. I don't know if any of the guys could."

"Admitting that takes guts, too," Michelle commented.

"Listen to them." Sandy rolled her eyes. "That's real consideration, you guys, standing over our lunch table and talking about guts. Give us a break."

Michelle felt her face turn hot. That surprised her—she wasn't talking to Derek!

Sandy watched Matt leave. She patted Michelle's shoulder. "Somebody likes you," she said knowingly.

"Get real. He's part of the team."

"Yeah, the part that drew mustaches on your picture.

Now he feels horrible because he likes you."

"You don't know that."

"Do, too."

"Who says?"

"I do. He didn't have to come over here. He could have waited and said something to you before the game. I bet he's going to ask you to the movies this weekend."

Michelle crumpled her straw into her milk carton. She pushed back her chair. "Excuse me, but you need to play sports sometime. We're a team. We don't even think boy and girl stuff."

Across the table, Skye almost choked on her milk. "Matt still likes you."

Michelle scowled as both her friends doubled up with laughter. They howled even louder when she tossed her things in the wrong recycling bins on her way out of the cafeteria.

Coach and the boys were waiting for the girls after school in the boys' locker room. He motioned them to sit down.

"Remember everything we covered in practice. Each of you has strengths and weaknesses that you bring to this game. But everyone needs a little help sometime. Be alert to hear calls for passes from your teammates. It's teamwork that wins in basketball."

More serious this time, they pulled their skullcaps on and formed their circle with bald heads bowed and hands extended.

"Go, Eagles!"

They ran through a wall of noise and into the gymnasium. Flashbulbs popped. Just as he had said he would, Brian knelt at the entrance with his camera.

"Michelle!"

Michelle gave him a thumbs up and kept moving.

Down court, the Barracudas in their mean silver and red uniforms looked more like steamrollers than a basketball team. Right away, she spotted the three Barracuda girls, all big, all muscular. If her stomach ever stopped churning, it would be a miracle.

Michelle glanced at Derek. She thought he must have noticed her sick expression because he winked. At the same time, Stephanie and the cheerleaders began a high-kicking cheer.

"Derek, Derek, he's our man, if he can't do it, then Smidge can."

Hot, Michelle took the ball and let it fly. A loud shriek filled the air when it dropped in the basket.

"Way to go, Michelle!"

Michelle grinned. She recognized Sandy's voice.

Feeling braver, Michelle searched the stands until she found her parents sitting with Skye's mom. She gave them the A-OK sign with her fingers and thumb just as the warning whistle sounded.

"Okay, guys," Coach said. "Let's get on the boards. Keep the ball moving until you can get a good shot at the basket. Derek, you cover Number 11. If you can't guard her, I'll give that position to someone else. Let's see what you can do."

With their pompoms resting quietly on their hips, the cheerleaders stood at attention as Derek and a flashy girl

Barracuda with long black braids approached the center ring for the initial jump ball. All eyes focused on Derek as he crouched, ready to spring. The referee blew the whistle and tossed the ball in the air.

"Yea, Derek!"

Derek tapped the ball to Julio, who pivoted, waiting for Derek to cut around for the pass as Keisha and Michelle dashed down court. Suddenly coming from nowhere, a Barracuda guard whipped inside, picking up Julio's bounce pass in the process.

Right away, the Barracudas began a fast break. After they passed the ball, they ran at full speed for their basket. Two points went up on the Barracudas' side of the board and the game had hardly even started!

Derek took the ball out. Michelle ran a zigzag pattern that left her guard in the dust, took Derek's pass, faked left, and dribbled toward Keisha, who caught her bullet pass as Michelle kept moving toward the basket. Any other team might have been fooled. Not the Barracudas. True to their name, two hungry Barracuda guards wasted no time honing in on Keisha. Michelle could almost feel Keisha's goose bumps as she met the challenge head-on.

Pa-boom-pa-boom-pa-boom. Keisha danced backward with the ball playing its sweet music. *Pa-boom-pa-boom-pa-boom.*

With her free hand, Keisha beckoned both guards. "Come to me, baby. You want this ball? Here you go. Take it. Take it."

Then, just as the first guard lunged, she faked, sending the other guard in the opposite direction. Just as quickly, she reversed and swerved around both of them, sinking a basket with an awesome hook shot.

The Jefferson fans went wild.

Derek's Barracuda, the girl with the braids, took the ball out. She passed and cut around smoothly, while the receiving Barracuda dribbled expertly down the court. The Eagle guards kept their arms out as they tried to block pass after pass, but the ball went to another hungry fish who shot the ball effortlessly into the basket.

Coach took Michelle and Keisha out, substituting Bob and Steve. Later, Matt went in for Derek. Skye got to play, too. Rocco came out. Coach kept all the players rotating, making sure no one became too tired.

Bob made a quick pass to Steve, who leaped high in the air for a two-handed catch. Whoa! From there, the ball went to Skye for a set shot and two points, bringing the score to 16-12, Barracudas' favor.

Coach tapped Michelle, sending her and Rocco back into the game.

No doubt about it, the Barracudas played a shrewd game. As they put the ball in motion, Rocco's Barracuda moved closer to Michelle, bringing Rocco along with him. If they didn't watch out, they'd collide for sure. Michelle nodded to Rocco, then smoothly picked up his guy, leaving Rocco to pick up hers—an incredibly fast Barracuda *girl*.

"Good moves!" Coach shouted from the sidelines.

Just then the pass went to Michelle's Barracuda. Michelle dove after the ball, but she wasn't quick enough. The next pass went to Rocco's Barracuda girl, right under the basket. Rocco's arms went up as he tried to block the shot.

Box her out! Michelle screamed silently. As the ball went in the air, Rocco pivoted. But instead of crouching and boxing the girl out with his arms and rear, he stood scared, straight and tall. Seizing the moment, the Barracuda whipped around Rocco, grabbed the rebound, and stuck it back into the air and down into the basket.

Rocco shuffled his feet and groaned.

"It's okay, big guy. You'll get her next time." Michelle pretended it didn't matter when, of course, it mattered a lot.

The Barracudas played a mean game of ball. The next two times the Eagles had the ball, the Barracudas stole it, once from Michelle and once from Bob. Both times they added more points to their side of the scoreboard.

"Keisha, here!" Bob shouted.

Keisha passed the ball to Bob, who dribbled swiftly along the sideline before passing the ball to Derek for a layup. The ball hit the rim. *Broing!*

A girl Barracuda recovered it. She heaved the ball far down court to a teammate who, in the blink of an eye, took it in for another two points. Barracudas 24, Eagles 18. Ouch! The Eagles were getting their feathers clipped!

Toward the end of the first half, the Barracudas went into a frustrating zone defense. Losing patience fast, Derek charged.

"Foul! Two shots!" the referee called.

Flipping her braids over her shoulders, Derek's Barracuda strolled to the foul line. Both shots sailed in with a smooth swish. The muscles in Derek's jaws tensed. His fists clenched and unclenched angrily as the buzzer sounded for half time.

"Okay, guys," Coach said in the locker room. "We're only five baskets in the hole. Let's beef up our defense and accelerate our offense. Let's drown those Barracudas. You can do it!"

The teams warmed up at opposite ends of the court and resumed play.

The tap went to Steve. A few minutes later, the Barracudas blew into Skye as she moved the ball cautiously along the sidelines. Thinking fast, Skye sent the ball rolling across the floor to Michelle.

Her Barracuda guard bent over Michelle so closely, she could smell the onions he'd had for lunch. She was trapped! And what a smelly defense!

Michelle leaned forward, protecting the ball when she really wanted to fan the fumes. Just then Matt shot by in front of her with his hands cupped to form a target, his fingers spread out and ready to grip the ball. Quickly, she handed the ball off to him. What a save! She was out of a tight and smelly spot and Matt was in for the basket.

Barracudas' ball, but not for long. Bob stole it. Suddenly, Skye tumbled to the floor. Two free throws.

"Just like in the driveway, Skye. You can do it." Michelle held her breath as Skye bounced the ball three times, gave it a push, and let it fly. *Swish!* The stands went crazy.

Michelle raked her bangs up off her forehead with her fingers. "One more, Skye. One more."

Looking nervous, Skye bounced the ball twice and sent it toward the basket. It bounced high against the rim and back into her hands.

"Skye! Signal timeout!" Coach shouted.

Immediately, Skye cradled the ball to her chest and motioned to the referee. "Time out!" she yelled, loud enough that everyone in the gymnasium heard.

"Okay, team. Listen up!" Coach said in the huddle. "We're going to box out on the next rebound. When you take the ball down for the basket, the moment you shoot, I want Rocco, Derek, and Skye to get in front of your players and box them out. That'll give you a better chance at recovering the ball. We can't win unless we have the ball."

Michelle glanced at Keisha. She made a tight fist and socked it into the palm of her other hand.

"Yes!"

When Michelle turned, she saw the Barracudas had used the timeout to good advantage. They sent in their three powerhouse players, all girls.

"Put it to 'em, Rocco!"

Rocco looked at her and grinned sheepishly.

"Do it!" From the bench, she emphasized her words with two fists, trying to give Rocco as much of her confidence as she possibly could.

Rocco pursed his lips. She'd never seen The Incredible Bulk so unsure.

Smooth as silk, the Eagles moved the ball toward their basket. As the ball went up, Derek, Rocco, and Skye crouched in perfect box-out positions, blocking the Barracudas from the rebound. Rocco's Barracuda girl stepped back, stunned by what had happened. In less than a second, Skye went from looking like a human coat hanger to a sleek airborne rocket. She leaped and tapped the ball to Ed, who sent it flying down court to Julio for two points.

On the sidelines, Coach beamed.

All right! What moves! The fired-up Eagles made it happen!

The next few plays worked well for the Eagles. For a while the score seesawed as both coaches rotated their players.

Michelle went in for Keisha.

A few minutes later, the Eagles lost the ball to the Barracudas, who froze it to protect their slim lead. Instead of going for a basket, the Barracudas knocked valuable seconds off the clock by passing only to each other, usually to the girls. Suddenly, Michelle saw a silver and red blur fly past her face.

The referee's whistle shrilled. "Jump ball!"

Steve and the Barracuda girl stepped into the center ring.

Steve tapped the ball. For a minute it looked like the Eagles might sink it. But then it went back to the Barracudas.

"DE-fense . . . *clap-clap* . . . DE-fense . . . *clap-clap* . . . DE-fense," the Eagle spectators demanded as they turned their volume up high.

Coach signaled timeout to call for an all-court press defense. The score was 34-33, Barracudas' favor. "You Eagles have to get that ball back *now!*" he said. "Go after the guy who has the ball. Don't let up. The team that has the ball and sinks the next basket is the team that wins."

Michelle glanced at the clock. Fourteen seconds. They couldn't lose by one lousy point. They just couldn't!

"Make this your win," Coach said.

Matt, Derek, Keisha, Skye, and Michelle returned to the floor as the fans rocked the rafters.

A Barracuda girl passed to another Barracuda, who—

Michelle exploded. She snatched the ball before the Barracuda saw it coming and raced down court.

A miss! They lost the ball again.

Ten seconds. The kids in the stands began counting the clock down.

"Ten . . . nine . . ."

A Barracuda sent the ball up for an easy shot and missed, but already Skye was soaring. She snatched the rebound, bounced it to Derek, who lobbed it to Michelle. Her thumbs close together and behind the ball, she chest passed it to Matt. He pivoted and sent it flying toward the goal.

"Five . . . four . . ."

Bing! It only slightly tapped the backboard before catching the rim. For a second, the air seemed sucked out of the gym as everyone stopped counting to hold their breath.

"Oooh," everyone groaned as the ball dropped outside the basket.

Blue and gold clashed with silver and red as bodies soared for the ball. Keisha grabbed it and sent it back up— and in for the winning basket! Jefferson Junior High let loose with an earsplitting scream.

"ONE! ZERO!"

The final buzzer sounded.

Michelle stumbled to a stop. She could barely see the scoreboard through the swirls of confetti. It landed every-where—on her shoulders, in her hair, on the floor. Suddenly Matt was beside her, squeezing her hand while all around them it snowed blue and gold.

CHAPTER 15

As suddenly as Matt touched her hand, he disappeared, leaving Michelle standing alone in the screaming crowd.

The scoreboard showed 35-34, an Eagles victory.

They had won by one point because they played as a team. Did the boys, Matt included, realize that? Everyone played well, but did they understand that Skye's free throw followed by her excellent rebound and grace under pressure had turned the game around? Keisha made the final point, but it took Matt, Michelle, and Derek to get Keisha in position. They played hard and as equals, but was that good enough to continue as a team?

With her towel draped around her neck, Michelle worked her way through the throng toward the girls' locker room.

But just as she leaned her back against the door, she saw Matt waving her into the boys' locker room, grinning from ear to ear.

Michelle looked both ways. She ducked her head to

go under his arm and then followed him inside toward the benches.

"Everyone else is here," Derek called out, seeing her. "We were afraid we'd lost you, Smidge."

She didn't know how, but Matt's grin had spread even wider. "Yeah, we got something for the whole team."

Suddenly suspicious, Michelle stepped back.

She'd seen the pros' locker rooms on TV when the players sprayed each other with bottles of champagne. She also remembered the rumors about eighth graders. What better time for the guys to throw her, Skye, and Keisha in the shower or spray them with soda pop?

She eyed the boys cautiously. They had their hands hidden behind their backs.

So did Coach.

"Uh-oh." When Michelle stepped back, ready to run, she bumped into Skye.

"Surprise!" the boys yelled.

Matt, Derek, Coach, and the rest of the guys whipped Groucho Marx eyeglasses with bushy eyebrows and black mustaches from behind their backs and placed them on their faces.

Then Derek stepped forward to stand beside Coach. One by one, Coach handed three more disguises to Derek, who in turn placed them on Keisha, Skye, and finally Michelle.

They all had mustaches!

Derek waved his fingers in front of his face. He made his bushy eyebrows go up and down. "Welcome to the new and totally awesome Eagles," he said in his best

Groucho imitation.

Michelle tried to cover her mouth to keep from laughing or crying—she didn't know which. But her mustache got in the way. It didn't matter.

Behind them, she heard Brian's hearty laugh as purple and red flashbulbs exploded in front of her face. Memories of the Eagles. Pictures for the yearbook.

"GO-OOOOO, TEAM!"